Dead Lucky

By

Francis G. Manley

Shield  Crest

© Copyright 2009 F. G. Manley

All rights reserved

This book shall not, by way of trade or otherwise, be lent, re-sold, hired out, or otherwise circulated without the prior consent of the copyright holder or the publisher in any form of binding or cover other than that in which it is published and without a similar condition including this condition being imposed on the subsequent purchaser

ISBN: 978-0-9558557-3-3

MMIX

Published by
ShieldCrest,
UK: Aylesbury, Buckinghamshire, HP22 5RR
USA: Morrisville, NC 27560
www.shieldcrest.co.uk

Reeling from the shock of losing her husband in a tragic motor accident, Lisa gets another surprise when she discovers he was leading a double life.

It is only later that she realizes that her husband had purchased the winning ticket in the weekly national lottery…and then remembers that he was buried with it!

Lisa enlists help and sets about retrieving the valuable ticket. But doing so unintentionally sends her headlong into a dangerous criminal underworld that will take all of her wits to survive in the heart-stopping adventure of **Dead Lucky**.

Other books by the author

"The Great Art Scam."

A children's 'teen' story, featuring the Telling Twins..

First published in 2004

CHAPTER 1

Martyn Whittle did what he always did on a Friday, called in at Desmond's Newsagents, at give or take a minute or two after six, filled in one line of a lottery ticket, and instructed Roly behind the counter to complete another two, by way of lucky dip. Then, buying a scratch card, he rubbed off the symbols. Disappointed once again, he turned to leave the shop.

Roland Desmond smiled sympathetically, and did what he'd done scores of times before, bringing his finger to his throat and making the usual cut throat mime.

Martyn grinned back in a silent consensus.

"Never mind, hey! I'll crack it one day you mark my words," he said, folding the terminal receipt ticket into his own, then placing them into the inside pocket of his blazer.

Slamming the door… the bell sang out noisily behind him.

Friday, was also the day of the week, that he chose not to go straight home.

Leaving his BMW in the Centre Grove multi-storey; he walked the two blocks of buildings to Lanions, the Florist shop in the High Street.

It had become a sort of habit. Knowing that if he wanted, he could park outside the shop after six. But he still had a hangover from that dramatic day when a ticket had defaced his windscreen, signed by the little ex-army man nicknamed the corporal, Penington's over zealous traffic warden.

Shaking off the unpleasant memory, he used his own key to let himself in at the side door, before climbing the thirteen steep steps of a carpet-less staircase to the first of two small flats, on the second- floor landing.

Nicol had already heard him come up, and was standing with the apartment door ajar, vigorously brushing out a handful of her long, lustrous auburn hair.

"A full furlough or short stay?" she asked, lowering her arms, taking his hand, and leading him into the lounge.

"Don't be greedy lass we can't do it two weekends on the trot." he replied, conversely memorising, how wonderful it had been staying the two and half days from Friday to Sunday, the previous weekend.

"I told you before, Phillip can only cover for me once a month, he's even got the works accountant entering a fictional expense account for the tax man, anyway Lisa has been asking me more than the usual amount of questions lately, so I'd better watch it on that front." he added.

"Well why don't you do the honourable thing then? leave her... broke and stony, and come over to me. Just think we could make a name for ourselves in some production, or other, work eight days a week and become household names." Nicol teased.

Knowing that her veiled sarcasm would inevitably bring out his rebellious nature, and get him to chatter more. She was always probing, trying to find out where his heart lay, testing him to see whether it was her he really wanted or, as it seemed most of the time, using her as some kind of accessory for his real passion, acting.

The bottom line as far as she was concerned was, why hadn't he left his wife yet?

But Martyn had lived out this scenario a hundred and one times in the past, and he wasn't going to be drawn this time either, on the other hand he couldn't help but think, if it hadn't been for Lisa's aversion to him spending all his spare time at Penington's Drama club, along with all those ultimatums, he probably wouldn't have cheated, and perhaps even never had met the beautiful Nicol, who fuelled and fired his rebellious nature.

Anyway, he thought, that's water under the bridge now. All he could really hope for was not to get caught, and continue having the best of both worlds, albeit a Jekyll and Hyde existence, a place of his own making... he had furtively lived in, for over a year now.

Once the length of his stay was established, Lisa who had also become a creature of habit, did exactly what Martyn would have expected, without a by your leave she slipped her stylish, red, three quarter tartan coat around her shoulders, then slipped silently out through the door.

Hope she gets the kebabs this time, he thought. A couple of times lately, he'd had to settle for that awful curried chicken, it depended on whether Lorenzo's was open or not.

While waiting he went into her bedroom and rummaged through the wardrobes, looking for his grey pin stripe, a double breasted suit, the prop suit he was using in the current production at Mill Brook Hall, the old dilapidated theatre building the society used for rehearsals

This week they were rehearsing Tennessee Williams' 'The Glass Menagerie.' And he couldn't help but notice that Nicol had been somewhat premature, her nineteen forties dress and accessories were lying neatly on the bed, overlaid with her black suspenders and nylon stockings neatly folded on top. Martyn felt his pulse accelerate, a vivid picture of Nicol loomed into his mind, with her nymph like voluptuous body encased in the garments.

Instinctively, he sat down on the edge of the bed caressing them surrendering to warm growing feelings of desire.

Suddenly he was shocked back into reality, she had returned and he could hear her clinking plates out in the kitchen.

"Are you going to eat or not?" she shouted.

"Yes... yes." he called back feeling like a guilty schoolboy having naughty thoughts.

"I'm coming." he said again, glancing at his watch, which told him there was only just over a half an hour left before rehearsals.

He wished he'd had more time.

Martyn wolfed down the kebabs, dipping them into Lorenzo's special sauce, and in his haste nearly pieced his lip with the meat stake.

Nicol came out of the bedroom, looking gorgeous wearing a shiny black Mac, that covered up her forties prop costume.

"What time's the cab?" she asked.

"Same time as usual...a quarter to... look, I won't have time to change now, you go down and I'll grab the script and things and change at rehearsals." he directed.

When they finally arrived at the theatre they were five minutes late, and true to form Jeremy, the director, ripped straight into them as soon as they stepped onto the stage area.

"Can't you keep to the clock, surely you both know by now I have a three week deadline for this production... and two bloody weeks have disappeared in to a black abyss already." he screamed.

Neither Martyn nor Nicol said anything. They knew by bitter experience that Jeremy, a former life-long professional actor, was a highly strung perfectionist, and to make any comment now would be tantamount to interrupting the Queen, making a state of the nation speech

Martyn nervously excused himself to the toilet in order to change his clothes, luckily he had on an anorak, that concealed his day clothes, otherwise the highly-strung luvvy would have yet another excuse to clobber him, he thought.

Later that evening, when the rehearsal was over, Martyn reflected that perhaps Jeremy's attitude, going on like he had, was a good thing after all. It had created a lot of deep seated anger inside him, which made him act out his part, of the cynical son doing battle with his deluded mother, with reams of life- like emotion.

Everybody there remarked that his interpretation of the character was the best yet, the way he had handled 'Tom's emotional show down' with sister Laura, played by Nicol, was as good as any pro could have portrayed it.

Even Jeremy came over to him afterwards, and right there, in front of the cast, he vigorously shook his hand, saying he couldn't have played the part better his self.

Coming from the old pro, that was praise indeed, thought Martyn.

Not so Nicol, she had a face like a deflated tyre, which worried him a lot.

He pondered why, as he followed her out of the theatre still wearing his prop clothes.

Before returning to the flat, they called in at the Queens Head for a drink, and what should have been a happy social occasion, was rapidly turning into a battle of wills. Nicol kept sounded him out, asking him why he hadn't dumped Lisa yet.

At first he thought she was making a point, with her usual playful nature, he had been feeling upbeat all night, especially with all the praise he had received from the other members of the cast. Perhaps he'd got a little too high- spirited, arrogant even, maybe that was the reason. She was obviously trying to take the wind out of his sails and knock him down a peg or two.

Later, when they arrived back at her flat, they both remained silent.

Martyn hadn't seen Nicol in this kind of serious mood before, she seemed extremely depressed, and try as he may he couldn't recall her being so adamant about leaving his wife, ever since they had first met.

He would try to save the situation… work his charm. It had worked on lots of occasions in the past.

Nicol had gone into the bedroom to change, Martyn opened up a bottle Shiraz.

He knew she wouldn't be able to resist this, it was her favourite, he mused, as he filled up two large glasses. Sauntering into the lounge he switched on the Hi- Fi, and placed her favourite Patsy Kline CD. on the tray of the machine.

As if on cue Nicol opened the bedroom door. She was scantily clad, her auburn hair, which earlier had been tied back, was now hanging long and loose, half covering her pert upturned breasts below which, her milky white nakedness perfectly honed downwards, accentuating the swell of her voluptuous rounded hips.

Underneath she wore an old fashioned girdle, which held up her wrinkled nineteen- forties nylon stockings, hooked onto a black suspender belt.

Martyn, literally dropped the glass of wine he'd been holding, the blood-red liquid spattering over the carpet and his shoes.

He had thought he would be the one to make the running, but she surprised him yet again, as he instinctively bent down and made an attempt to clean up the spill.

"Forget that darling that can wait, but I can't," she said, in a purring voice, no louder than a whisper.

The power of desire overwhelmed him as his lips found hers, he forced her quivering mouth apart his tongue venturing inside caressing hers, his hand behind, squeezing and caressing the nape of her neck.

No words were uttered as they collapsed down onto the pink sheets. In lustful haste they wrestled for position. Nicol fought for, and won the dominant stance, tugging Martyn's hair she forced his head down over the side of the mattress.

Astride him now, she undid his belt freeing him for their pleasure, then sinking her mouth onto his she bit his bottom lip, drawing blood, causing Martyn to cry out.

She plunged her shapely loins astride his willing body, continuously moving up and down and side to side, until the wanton power of love and desire possessed them.

The lust of the moment drowned them both in a screaming frenzy of emotion that words can only attempt to describe.

Separated again, they lay side by side lapsing into a sepulchral silence, cooling now, their fever spent.

"That really was something else," Martyn said, blindly reaching down to the floor for his trousers, fumbling for his pack of cigarettes.

"True, but how many times have you said that...is that what you keep saying to her too...?" Nicol quizzed, sneeringly.

"Don't be daft, you know that died a death a long time ago, what the hell's the matter with you tonight Nic?" Martyn asked, taken aback with her dogged determination.

"How do I know it has died a death," she spat back,

"You say that but… you're still living with her, still taking to her, look Martyn darling, Lisa's not the only one who can issue ultimatums... it's my turn this time, if you don't leave her by the end of one week, you can say goodbye to me forever...do you understand?"

He gave up searching for his cigarettes, feeling a rush of angry emotion take control of him, his chin shaking uncontrollably.

Jumping up off the bed he rammed his legs violently into his trouser legs, then snatching his shirt, jacket and shoes he crashed out of the room, saying nothing, as he slammed the door shut, like someone demented.

Fortunately, the street was sparsely populated as he marched in the direction of the multi-storey to pick up his car. Had anyone been near him then, they would surely have been a little apprehensive as he wrestled with his shirt and jacket, swearing out loud and venting anger on anything and everything that moved.

Pressing his foot down harder on the accelerator, the power of the sixteen- valve fuel injection engine seemed to respond even faster than his thoughts.

He didn't normally use the narrow, farm lane route, but he knew that if he cut through the countryside by way of Beakers Grove, it would take a good fifteen minutes off his journey home.

He felt tortured inside, his mind in turmoil. Another ultimatum! This time surprisingly, from Nicol of all people. What is it with women, he thought, they always end up wanting to set the agenda, especially if they think they had won the emotional ground.

With tyres screeching out on each bend of the narrow, poorly lit road, Martyn didn't see the articulated trailer parked up near the farm gate, until it was too late.

He knew a collision was inevitable; It was like he was entering a dark, one way tunnel, the wrong way. Using all the strength he could muster he wrestled with the steering wheel, trying to pull the car over to the right, and at the same time, ramming the foot brake down to the floor.

Even though he felt it was too late, his final thoughts were optimistic. Maybe he'd get hurt, but if his luck held out, he could survive even this.

The tyres screeched and the car skidded out of control, rolling over twice before screeching to a shuddering halt, ending up on its roof.

His twisted body had been thrown clear, but to no avail.

He lay there on his back in the damp grass, his lifeless eyes staring up to a galaxy of twinkling stars, in the cold black sky.

There was a minute and a half of deathly… eerie silence, before the sound of a ground-shaking explosion… followed by a blazing inferno.

CHAPTER 2

Lisa didn't wait up for him to come home, she had at the start of their troubles, but it always ended up in a fight.

She had got used to him arriving back in the small hours, but lately she just didn't care, after all she had a job too, albeit part time, and needed her sleep. So it was no surprise to hear the front door bell in the early hours, he'd probably forgotten his keys again, just as he had on a number of occasions recently.

Looping the cords around her dressing gown she descended the stairs slowly, trying to shape what she was going to say. Not wanting any of those awful arguments, and the children disturbed in the small hours.

Opening the door she was surprised to see a policewoman, and directly over her shoulder, she noticed a young constable getting out of the panda car.

"Are you Mrs Whittle...Lisa Whittle?" the young woman asked.

"I am." Lisa replied. "What's wrong...has something has happened, why are you here?

It's my husband...isn't it?"

"I'm afraid there's been a accident, involving a car, we weren't absolutely sure who was involved, so we done a check with the vehicle licensing centre at Swansea ...and I'm afraid we came up with your husband's name and address," he said.

"Is he hurt... in hospital?" she asked, tears beginning to cloud her eyes.

"I'm afraid the man, whoever he was, is beyond help, he's dead Marm" the young policeman said, quietly, standing now alongside his colleague.

Lisa wobbled for a couple of seconds, losing her balance, as if in a faint, the young man leapt forward to help prop her up, suggesting they go inside and sit down.

On their way through the lounge, the policewoman noticed a drink cabinet situated underneath a window, and asked if she could get her something.

Lisa nodded, mumbling that she needed a Vodka and lemonade.

"I don't suppose there could be any mistake could there," she pleaded, trying hard to hold back a flood of tears.

"Well...er' that's the trouble really ...there was an explosion..." the young policeman said in a quiet voice, trying his best to take the drama out of his description.

"Perhaps someone else was driving, d'you know of anyone that would drive his car?" he added.

Lisa shook her head negatively.

"Well I'm afraid we'll need you to identify the body, and some of the artefacts that were left on the scene," he explained.

Lisa fell forward, her body folding over from the waist down, making her long blonde hair cascade downwards to shroud her knees, sobbing now, with the full realisation of what really happened, the awfulness of the words explosion and fire, bringing it well and truly home to her.

"Look, Mrs Whittle have you got any close relatives...someone who could keep you company, stay the night perhaps... we could get in touch with?" the policewoman asked, helping her to raise the tumbler to her lips.

"There's only my sister but she lives down south...I'll have to let her know, I have a friend, Donna- Marie... Donna Gale, my partner at the shop...the woman I work with, she would stay with me." Lisa said, having difficulty getting her breathe between the words.

"Shall I phone her for you?" the policewoman suggested.

"Yes." Lisa replied, pointing to where her personal number book was to be found.

While she telephoned, the young constable told her she could wait until tomorrow for the identification, he suggested that they could stay with her until her friend arrived, but would have to report back to the station later.

Lisa felt a feeling of anxiety well up inside her, she dreaded the thought of having to wait until morning with that kind of uncertainty, even with her friend as company. blurted out.

"No! I want to do it tonight, I have to find out if it is Martyn, it would be hell not knowing. Perhaps there's a chance that it's not him... do you understand?"

"Of course yes, that's all right madam, if you feel you are up to it, but I think it best to warn you it won't be a pretty sight," he replied, firmly.

The young policewoman agreed to stay at the house to make sure the children weren't disturbed.

Fifteen minutes later Donna Marie screeched to a halt outside the house in her noisy old Metro, Lisa ran to the door and let her in, she noticed her friend had packed a holdall, which was only half zipped, leaving a frilly pink night-dress hang out, trailing along the floor.

"Oh! Lisa love what can I say, you don't deserve this…I'll stay as long as you want me to," Donna said, taking her into her arms, hugging and consoling her.

"Are you sure it's Martyn, going by what they said on the phone, they don't seem so positive about it either," she added, realising instantly, that she wouldn't receive an answer.

Her friend had literally collapsed into her arms, like a lifeless rag doll.

Half an hour or so later the three of them left in the police car, making their way to the Penington General Hospital in the centre of town.

The policeman had stopped the car outside the pathology building, and then mentioned casually, that they had already got in touch with her husband's business partner, a Mr Phillip Marks, as this wasn't a straightforward case of identification.

The young policeman's words may have been routine to him, but to Lisa, they were tantamount to someone hurling a brick through a plate glass window, it was as if the devil was trying to complete the job that he had started.

She resolved there and then, to avoid him at all cost.

Martyn had caught the force of an explosion on the left side of his body, his right side was virtually untouched, except for some bruises and abrasions caused by the impact.

Even being warned and prepared for the experience, couldn't stop Lisa gasp in horror when she finally realised it was him.

They asked her to look again to confirm an old injury above his right ankle.

She took a deep breath, and managed on the second occasion to identify a scar just above his ankle on the right leg.

The scar, ironically, was caused by another road accident they had been involved in, a few months before they had got married, his foot had very nearly been severed after a collision with, of all things, a milk float, after he had got it jammed beneath the accelerator pedal.

"He was in hospital for over a week after that so it must be in his medical records," Lisa said, with an air of resignation, and being supported by her friend.

Later, as they left the pathology building, Donna heard the sound of a vehicle pulling up behind them, she turned and saw another police car stop at the entrance port of the building they had just walked through, and realised the tall dark, slim moustachioed man, getting out of the car was Phillip Marks, she had met him once before, but thought it prudent not to mention anything to her friend, still in a sad world of her own, and very shocked.

When they finally arrived home the young policewoman reported that the children hadn't even stirred, then excused her self, explaining that she and her colleague would have to get back to the station to make out the report of the night's events, as they had received a report of another local fatality.

Lisa nor her friend didn't sleep a wink that night, instead they polished off a half bottle of Martyn's whisky, three quarters of a bottle of Vodka, and two bottles of red wine, every drop of booze they could find in the house.

The phone rang twice in the early hours, and each time Donna picked up the receiver no one answered, but she had a strong sense there was someone on the other end of the line. Each time her tearful friend asked who the caller was, Donna explained it was a wrong number, hoping it wouldn't occur again, making her excuse less credible each time. Her intuition told her that it was a man on the end of the line, but she dare not reveal her thoughts to her friend.

It was just after Eleven o' clock the following morning, when Bill and her sister Toni, arrived from Plymouth, they only stayed an hour or so, their main task being, to take the children back with them until Martyn's funeral the following Thursday.

"How are they taking it?" Toni asked.

"It's gone over the top of Ben's head, he's too young to understand, but Kirsty's been crying all morning, she's seven now and beginning to realise the gravity of things,"

Lisa explained, tears beginning to cloud over her eyes again.

She felt relieved when they decided not to stay too long, yet guilty because she wanted them to go. She would miss the children but knew they were in safe loving hands.

"Bill and I will see what we can do with them, now don't worry too much. See you on Thursday then." was the last thing Toni said, before driving off, the children looking confused and forlorn, as they waved half-heartedly through the rear window.

The following Monday, there was a letter from the coroners office stating the time and date of the inquest, adding there would be a automatic post mortem. They added that they envisaged no problems with the cause of death, as it was plainly accidental, so had no objections to the funeral going ahead on a date she'd yet to arrange.

Later that day, Jeremy Macklin the director of the Drama club came around and presented Lisa with a parcel of Martyn's clothes taken from his locker at the theatre.

Lisa, was surprised with the clothes she was given, she had assumed he'd been wearing this same outfit at the time of the accident, she clearly remembered him wearing his blazer and grey flannel trousers when he had left for work that Friday morning.

Querying Jeremy about this, he said he couldn't really remember seeing him changing into his prop clothes that Friday evening, but he recalled giving him and Nicol a rocket, as he put it, about being late, at the time he had assumed Martyn had turned up for rehearsals wearing his prop outfit.

Then he went on to say something odd.

"Nicol gave me the clothes the day before yesterday, I remember because, she said, they had a row that evening and he'd left the theatre with his prop clothes still on."

Lisa's mind slipped into top gear with this statement, for months past she suspected he'd been seeing someone, his behaviour had become strange, to say the least, but whenever she brought up the subject, he told her not be so silly.

This was the first real clue she had.

Donna made most of the arrangements for the funeral, taking place the following Thursday.

The undertaker had suggested cremation, but had shunned away from the suggestion, knowing the state of mind her friend was in, so on Lisa's orders she took his Blazer, and his grey flannel trousers to the undertakers. These were his favourite clothes, and Lisa was adamant, that he should be buried in them.

The day before the funeral, Lisa spent most of the day in her bedroom sifting through Martyn's personal effects, she dreaded the thought of Phillip Marks calling around, but knew he would.

Just over an hour later, he did just that.

Lisa had given Donna strict instructions about turning him away, which she had done with her customary efficiency: explaining that everyone was down with the flu.

Asking her friend about his reaction, she said he didn't say anything, just walked away, but then had stopped, turned around and glanced back a number of times, shaking his head, obviously very puzzled.

"Why are you so paranoid about him." Donna asked.

"It's a long involved story really, but the man has been a curse to our marriage, I met him a short time before meeting Martyn, and being young and carefree I flirted with him a little, there was nothing meaningful about it, not as far as I was concerned. He was already married to Carol at the time, but he must have taken the experience more seriously to heart than I did, because even after Martyn and I were married, he continued to make passes at me...I'd see him occasionally, 'cos of the business connection, but the devious swine never gave up trying to corner me, he gave the impression that he wanted to posses me body and soul. The clown seems to have some kind of weird fixation with me.

Carol has left him since, two years ago in fact... taking the two kids, couldn't put up with anymore of his womanising, I shouldn't wonder.

Even when the children were born he'd still find ways to play his cunning games.

I got Martyn to have a word with him about it on more than one occasion, but he always threatened to break up the partnership.

That always frightened Martyn, the devious sod always made threats… if he was cornered, always threatening to pull the financial rug out from under us." Lisa explained.

In all the time Donna Marie had spent working with Lisa at their shop, she'd never had an inkling of this, Lisa had never let on, it really was a revelation, deep down she admired her for keeping her troubles to herself, but felt she had been left out in the cold, especially now, right at this moment…there was so much she could have done to help her.

"Why didn't you tell me," Donna quizzed.

"I thought I'd be able to cope…I always thought Martyn would see sense and dissolve the partnership, but he always insisted it was too late, our future depended upon it, he said he had invested too much of his life in the business to pull out."

Bill and her sister arrived up from Plymouth just before noon, on Thursday morning, the day of the funeral.

On the surface Kirsty and Ben seemed surprisingly normal and unemotional, except for a few tantrums and tears in the morning from little Ben who had caught sight of his Daddy's photograph in her bedroom. A snap taken at Disney World, Paris, the year before.

Lisa could have kicked herself for leaving it up there, she should have known that it would evoke some kind of reaction from the kids, especially Ben the sensitive one.

Now she felt completely empty, and strangely devoid of any emotion ever since she had got up that morning, and explained this feeling to her friend, who by now, had become a kind of confident helper and councillor to her.

Donna thought she was doing what any normal parent would do, blocking out the sad series of events out, subconsciously trying to protect the children.

She tried to help her by stressing after all the tears she had shed, that her need now, was to go on the offensive, take charge and get some measure of control.

Towards mid- morning the house was beginning to fill up with family members, not that there were many close one's left on Martyn's or Lisa's side.

Her father Eric Tinsley, and his second wife Barbara, had driven down from Altringham near Manchester, her real mother, Lydia, had died over twenty years ago now. There wasn't much of a family tie left now, just her step brother Zac, Barbara's son, who still lived at the same house with his father Eric and new wife.

Martyn's mother, a widow, in her late seventies, suffered from rheumatoid arthritis. She had great difficulty getting about; she had been a tall elegant looking lady, but now she was a shadow of her old self, sitting bent over in a wheelchair. She and her carer, had managed somehow to come all the way up from her nursing home down at Chelmsford, in Essex.

Lisa was glad she hadn't carried out her threat to tell the old lady about Martyn's behaviour in the heat of their many fights, now at least the old girl could say her goodbye's... thinking everything had been sweet and orderly between them.

At one thirty, the Reverend A. Ericson from the local United Reform Church accompanied the pall bearers and coffin into the lounge for a short service, she couldn't help but feel a bit of a hypocrite really, she nor Martyn had never been of any particular religious persuasion, they had both agreed earlier on in their marriage that the best label they could bestow on themselves would be as agnostics, and not really knowing what that meant really, and true to their word they never did have the children christened. But Donna who still attended church occasionally, had persuaded her to do the conventional thing.

With the twenty minute service over, the mile long drive in the lead car following the hearse to the Municipal cemetery, seemed to take an eternity, Martyn's mother sobbed quietly, all the way there. Toni and Bill did their best to try and calm the situation, taking turns to console her, placing their arms around the shaking shoulders of the grieving woman.

Lisa reflected about the fateful week, trying to make some sense of the events since the accident, but the more she thought, the more she found she was apportioning blame on herself, altering actual happenings in her mind...anything! To try and take away the awfulness of what had happened.

Switching off from her negative train of thought she gave her full attention to the children.

At the grave side Lisa's detached mood began to dissipate, the trigger wasn't Martyn's interment but the sight of the smug Phillip Marks standing in the crowd opposite, a tingle crept up her spine, in one fell swoop she realised how dangerous the future could be. There was no one left to take her part, to defend her, no one around to deflect him... She knew he would never give up now.

As soon as the service was over Lisa, drew Kirsty to her side and walked briskly back to the car, using her as a kind of shield, hoping he wouldn't approach her.

A traditional funeral fare of tea, wine and ham sandwiches, had been prepared and laid out by her neighbour Pam Yeo and her pretty young daughter Claire. Judging by the crowd of people arriving back at the house, Lisa wondered if there would be enough refreshments to go around.

Quite a large crowd of men had turned up, some of them obviously from Martyn's drama club, their badges displayed, alongside their black ties.

Lisa found herself searching for the mystery woman Nicol, she had never seen her, but after what Jeremy had said, the mysterious shadowy figure had haunted her thoughts all week long. She noticed the director talking to a small man in a group of people who, by now had spilled over into the kitchen, and told Donna to tell him that she'd like a word with him, realising if she tried to reach him herself, she'd would run into a wall of well meaning... but mind numbing sympathy. She just couldn't handle another dose of that right now.

It seemed to take ages for the tall, slim effete man to finally make his way over to her.

"What can I say that hasn't already been said Mrs Whittle," he said, holding a half-filled wine glass near his chin, as if in a kind of protective gesture in the overcrowded room.

"Martyn was a fine actor...a lovely man... the cast and I will miss him dearly." he added, his cold steel blue eyes avoiding hers, sweeping nosily around the room.

Lisa wondered if he would.

"Your current production was to start shortly… wasn't it?" Lisa asked with no real genuine interest, trying to lead him on towards her search for Nicol.

"Yes Nicol will have her work cut out she'll have to rehearse the whole thing with another leading man, it's going to put us back a week or two," he said, taking a giant swig from his glass, leaving it empty.

"I've had to arrange another deadline," he added, nodding to the back view of a slim auburn haired woman, standing alone, gazing through the patio doors, on their left,

That's her, Lisa realised, it must be her… but she would ask to be doubly sure.

Before she could, the director called the woman over.

Lisa noticed her mascara was smudged, her brown eyes tainted a bleary red. It was plainly obvious she had been in a bit of a state.

Nicol came over offering her hand, saying at the same time.

"I'm so sorry Mrs Whittle, we were scheduled to open the play early next week, as you know Martyn and I were the principles in this production,"

"No I didn't know." Lisa interrupted, sounding a little surly.

"We will all miss him," she added

"I bet you will." Lisa replied, hoping her obvious sarcasm would create some kind of reaction, but she didn't take the bait, she knew right away she was dealing with someone very devious.

At that moment Donna tapped her on the shoulder and whispered that Phillip Marks had turned up at the house, adding he had barged passed her like someone on an urgent mission, obviously searching for her.

Making her excuses, she turned away from Nicol, Jeremy and the others, and managed to slip quietly away from the crowded living room, using the side door from the lounge that led out into the hall. Ascending the stairs she entered her bedroom, making sure she locked the door behind her.

Later, realising that no one had attempted follow her, she crept gingerly down the stair-well again, trying to get the view of the lounge from the hallway. She caught site of him behind a group of people, sitting on a sofa, at the top end of the room, chatting to Nicol, of all people. His body language suggesting that this wasn't their first meeting. She determined he wouldn't see her, and rushed back upstairs to the sanctity of her bedroom again.

Donna came up to see her later, saying everyone had been asking for her, but most of them lost interest when she had made excuses about her friend not feeling well, now there were only a few of her family members left in the house.

Kirsty was helping Toni and Bill to wash up the dishes, later they volunteered to take the children back home with them for another week, if she so wished.

Lisa agreed she had a lot of loose ends to tie up, not least sorting out that business with the shady lady, she just had to know every detail of her relationship with Martyn.

Donna also agreed to stay another week, so by the time Toni and Bill and the kids were heading back south again, Lisa had a chance to take a deep breath and analyse the events of the day.

She knew she should be content to sit and reflect on this sad day, but a growing feeling of anger was beginning to overwhelm her, she decided to put these feelings to good use, and formulate a plan.

Martyn would still be alive if it hadn't been for that damn bitch. she thought.

So enlisting her friend's help, she spent the rest of the day, planning a strategy to track down the shady lady.

Early the following morning Donna drove to Jeremy's house at Upper Crayside, over in the east part of town, on the pretext of searching for a credit card that had belonged to Martyn, the real purpose being, to find Nicol's home address.

Lisa was adamant now that she had to lay the ghost to rest, perhaps then she and the children could make a start with the rest of their lives.

Her friend reported back a couple of hours later, saying she had enlisted Jeremy's help to search the old theatre building, and having no success there, he had volunteered to take her to Nicol's flat, in the town's high street, in case she had found it and taken it home.

But she wasn't at home, it had slipped his mind that the lady had a day job.

The problem being it was Friday night, and that was rehearsal night, so even if she returned, she wouldn't be home for long.

At five forty five, the same evening, Lisa parked her friend's Metro in a side street not far the town centre, she walked down into the high street and managed to install herself in the telephone kiosk, very nearly opposite Llanions the florist shop, the place Donna had described, pretending to use the phone.

Donna had told her that she lived up on the second floor, she hoped she'd got the right

She hadn't been in the booth two minutes when a large menacing looking man, in orange overalls tapped the Perspex shield, trying to mime amidst the noise of the traffic. He shouted that he needed to use the phone, but Lisa continued, pretending to use the phone. She had got an excellent vantage point, and wasn't going to surrender it, not until she caught sight of her mystery lady.

Five minutes later the pretty auburn haired woman wearing a three quarter tartan coat and red trews, fumbled in her handbag for keys. Finding them, she opened the door and entered the building by the side entrance of the shop, and after a short while, a tell- tale light appeared in a room above.

Lisa, slammed the phone down, and gave the irate man a unmistakable explicit finger sign, shouting,

"Here have the damn thing!" running across the busy road, and dodging the manic rush hour traffic to get to the shop.

Pressing the name button above the flat number 1A, she could plainly hear the telltale clipity clop sound, of steel high-heeled tips tripping down the carpet-less staircase.

The door opened slowly until it was stopped suddenly, held by a safety chain, but Lisa couldn't keep her composure any longer.

"Open the door you bitch," she shouted, "You know who I am, I'm Martyn's wife,"

"How did you find my address?" the frightened girl asked.

"Never mind that, let me in you slut," Lisa screamed again.

Ever since Martyn's demise, and especially the funeral, Nicol had been experiencing mounting feelings of guilt and remorse, and now, being confronted like this, fear began to overwhelm her, quickly making her become submissive.

Undoing the chain she knew it was time to come clean, it would be a relief to get this burden off her shoulders.

Nicol led the way up the stairs and into the flat.

"So this was your little love nest." Lisa said, taking in, and noting every detail of the small room. It was too late now, but in a perverse way it made her feel closer to Martyn....she just had to know everything.

Nicol tried to calm the situation offering Lisa a drink.

Lisa, taken aback accepted, but she knew before she had it in her hand she was about to do something outrageous, like throwing it back into her face…

And she did just that!… hurling the glass across the room, smashing it into a thousand pieces.

Nicol reacted by pushing her backwards, doubling Lisa's anger. Grabbing the hapless girl's hair, she dragged her across the length of the room into the kitchen, forcing her head down into the wash bowl, then turning the cold water tap on, she ordered the hysterical girl to tell her everything…or else!

Struggling in vain trying to get free, and feeling if she didn't, she would surely die.

Nicol agreed to tell her everything, if she would let her up first. Lisa loosened her grip and finally let her go, throwing her a towel, as she tried hard to regain her composure. Gasping deep breaths to try and calm herself a little, she mumbled something, that was hardly audible. It was now, that she could do with a drink.

It suddenly occurred to Lisa, that if a third party entered the room right there and then, and saw them, her… looking dishevelled behaving like some raving lunatic, and Nicol, with smudged panda eyes, and lipstick smeared across her face, They would be bound to conclude that it looked like a scene from a Stephen King horror movie.

"Look I don't how to say this without you attacking me again, but I loved him too, we wanted the same things, we even swapped rings, and he wore the one I bought him...he told me all about your ultimatums, and the fights you had," Nicol said, sobbing erratically.

"Never mind that you trollop he was a father of two beautiful children... didn't you ever give them any consideration, I bet you hardly knew they existed... when did it first start?... did you meet him at the club? Was it you who made the first move?" Lisa questioned."

"Yes, about two years ago," Nicol replied, hardly audible now.

"Oh! And incidentally, I saw you flirting with Phillip Marks at the funeral, have you laid him too?" she probed.

"We were friends a few years back." the dishevelled girl cried out.

"Friends?" Lisa probed again.

"Well it turned into a relationship later, his wife found out about it and left him, but that was before I met Martyn," the girl explained, "In fact he was the one who introduced me to Martyn in the first place," she added.

"The mercenary bastard!" Lisa exclaimed.

"Anyway he was the one who covered for the both of us with those business weekends." Nicol explained.

"My God that man is the devil incarnate," Lisa mumbled, understanding a lot more now.

"What?" Nicol asked, with a look of incredulity.

"You silly little bitch... you were just been a pawn in the game," Lisa spat back.

"I don't understand," the girl said, looking perplexed.

Lisa leapt up from her chair and grabbed her by the shoulders again, shouting,

"You don't need to, when I leave here I don't want to see your insipid little face again, but you are going to promise me something right here and now... Don't ever mention this conversation to Marks, if you do I'll swing for you... do you understand."

The frightened girl readily agreed, wanting nothing more to do with her or anyone who had connections with Martyn, she knew then, she was going to change her identity... and move a million miles away.

Lisa was still shaking when Donna opened the door, she walked straight past her, not speaking, and remaining silent for what seemed an eternity, before suddenly blurting out.

"It's ironical really I thought I'd exorcised the ghost but the Devil has sneaked up on me again."

"What devil?" Donna asked.

"Marks…Philip Marks… who else!" Lisa spat out, adding…

"I'm gonna make sure the partnership is well and truly scuppered …and then I'll probably move a hundred miles from here, you just watch,"

"You're not thinking clearly, let it stew for a while, can't you see you're letting him set the agenda." Donna interrupted.

Lisa thought her friend might just be right, so she busied herself sketching in all the details of what she had found out, hoping that by talking things through, she could plan something, and appease her raging anger.

CHAPTER 3

The following days felt like an anti climax to Lisa, Donna had retreated back to her home, but had agreed to manage the shop, until she had settled the children down to some semblance of normality.

Toni and Bill were due to bring the kids back up from Plymouth on Saturday morning.

The last couple of days of being truly alone had taken her to new depths, just touching some little thing Martyn had used, would be enough to spin her into a uncontrollable emotional whirlpool again.

Worst of all she had a nagging feeling of loss on two fronts, which was threatening to overwhelm her. Losing Martyn the way she had, coupled with yet another depressing feeling of loss concerning everything her heart had really desired, to the detestable Phillip Marks. It seemed to her that he had set out to destroy her from the very beginning, like a classic case of if he couldn't have her, no-one would.

Her obvious escape route would be to get away from everything familiar, and start life afresh somewhere else, but her friend had made the point, why should she allow him to set the agenda, yet at the same time, she knew she'd have to keep a door open for him in regards to dissolving the existing company arrangements.

That very morning in fact, there had been a letter from Peter Mason, the company solicitor, requesting a meeting with her and Marks in order to tie up some of the outstanding issues concerning the partnership. Her first thought was to delegate someone else, but on reflection she knew that wasn't possible, so she resolved to have as little contact with him as possible. If he dared make a move on her she would shoot him down in no uncertain terms.

On the Friday morning, Lisa decided to visit the cemetery before keeping her eleven o' clock appointment with Mason, right now she needed to talk with Martyn, hoping somehow he'd be listening, maybe there was just a chance that some part of him…a presence, a thought even, something that could help dissipate her mounting problems.

She had woke that morning feeling weary, having had only a few hours sleep, her mind in turmoil through the night, anticipating meeting Marks again, yet at the same time she knew she had to act responsibly, she needed to escape the situation with her dignity intact, as well as arranging some kind of financial settlement, for the children's future.

Martyn's grave was covered in myriad's of deciduous leaves, that had blown and drifted all over the cemetery from the tall elm, oak, and beach trees, bordering the huge municipal cemetery, It would be five weeks yet before the headstone is erected, she mused.

Her train of thought accentuated the sense of loss again, giving birth, to all too familiar feelings of loneliness and insecurity. Tears began to run uncontrollably down her cheeks again, glistening in the cold grey morning light.

'Oh! Why did this happen to us Martyn? When did it all start to go wrong … if we could only turn the clock back..." she sobbed out loud now, addressing her late husband.

An elderly man, wearing an old fashioned trilby hat, ambled by, his huge Alsatian straining on a leash, tipping his hat in her direction, he bid her good morning. Suddenly she felt shivery cold; the spell was broken, as she was catapulted back into the real world.

Bending down, she rearranged the crumpled wreaths, and brushed her warm moist eyes with the back of he cold hand

'Goodbye my love I'll be back to tell you what happened' she said quietly, before making her way back to Donna's battered old Metro.

Lisa hadn't seen the girl at the reception desk before, but it was obvious the girl had been briefed, because as soon as she introduced herself, she explained that they were expecting her in the office.

'They' it seemed, was the operative word, she mused, meaning her bogey- man was already there.

Her assumption proved correct, as soon as she had entered the office Marks said,

"Hello! Lisa, I've been trying to get in touch with you ever since the funeral, but that damned friend of yours, always gets in my way."

"Donna Marie you mean? Yes, she's a good friend but hardly damned, Lisa spat back.

"No, I didn't mean it like that, don't be so touchy, I just wanted to offer my sympathy, that's all, Martyn was my friend too you know," he said.

A thorn in your side- more like, Lisa thought.

Peter Mason cleared his throat, before interrupting,

"Can I offer you my deepest sympathy Mrs Whittle I hope you don't consider this meeting premature, but I must know if you and Mr Marks plan to keep the partnership going under a new arrangement, I understand he has already offered it to you verbally."

"Yes, but he and I know that I've already declined his offer, I have my own reasons, but I'd prefer to keep them to myself," Lisa answered, firmly.

"Look Lisa love, I've known you and Martyn from time immemorial, what's your problem?...you don't think you know enough about the software business, that's it... isn't it?" Marks interrupted.

Lisa was trying hard to keep up her facade of normal behaviour, for the sake of Mason and her own dignity, but now she was finding it more difficult by the second.

"So you want the business dissolved then," Mason cut in.,

Lisa nodded her agreement.

"Alright, I'll draw up the documents as soon as I get an independent accountant's report, I'll get on to it straight away, it should be ready in about a week,"

Mason explained.

"Look I don't want to appear rude but would that be all for now, I have some important business to attend to, shall we say another meeting in a week then, Lisa suggested.

Mason agreed, offering up his condolences again.

Relieved, she left the office in a hurry, hoping and praying Marks wouldn't follow, but he did, finally catching up with her in the foyer.

"What the hell's the matter with you, can't you see you're turning down a promising future, you could be a sleeping partner if you wanted... only attend company meetings when you wanted to...Look! my lady, I shouldn't be telling you this, but the company is in desperate need of finance, and you could say a lot of our troubles was down to Martyn. We had more than our share of trouble recently, one of our biggest customers let us down, and when the accounts are revealed...well, let's put it this way, I don't think you should expect a good settlement.

Now that your husband has gone... we could turn over a new leaf, 'er well... we both know he had a good life policy... couldn't you help," he said, not able to complete what he had started to say.

Lisa's fragile façade of normality finally cracked, her arm shot up like a displaced spring, the flat of her hand slamming into the right side of his face, leaving a crimson imprint from eye to jaw.

"Now d'you understand you creep... I wouldn't work with you if my life depended on it, I couldn't care less if you sink along with that blasted ship of yours, I can't stand being near you...you give me the willies." Lisa screamed.

The girl at reception had witnessed everything, frightened, and grabbing a handful of folders from the desk, she beat a hasty retreat to the offices at the rear.

Lisa rushed out into the street, leaving him shocked, and perplexed with a bemused look, etched across his face, as he stood there nursing his bruised jaw.

She felt full of rage but strangely relieved, the moment had been worth waiting for, she had wanted to punish the man for a long time now, this time the hurt was physical, and easily mended, but if there was to be a next time... she hoped she could wound his very soul.

It was plainly obvious to Donna, her friend was in a feverish temper, she knew her too well by now, and the habit of biting her bottom lip every second or so said everything.

"What ever is the matter?" She quizzed.

"I clobbered him, hurt him, I'm sure... but he'll be back for more, I just know it.

"Marks…I assume." He friend said knowingly.

Lisa nodded and went on to describe what had happened at Mason's.

Her friend looked surprised, saying,

"Good for you girl but after what you've told me I don't think he'll give up that easily either," before adding,

"Look darling I don't want to appear rude but there hasn't been that many punters today I've only had four customers all day, and two of them didn't buy anything. What do you say to coming around my house…for coffee or something, we could chat there, It'll help calm you down, I have to get home anyway, I'm expecting the gas people today, they're changing my meter for a new one…what d'you say?"

"OK it will make a change, anyway the kids will be back tomorrow, so I won't have much free time before long." Lisa replied.

Turning the corner into Cashmere Avenue, they observed a van parked outside the front gate, they were about to enter into the house, when a tall, good looking man, sporting a impressive Afro style haircut, ambushed them, startling the both of them.

"Mrs Gale?" he asked.

"Speaking!" Donna replied.

"Oh! I'm glad you turned up I can't do any work until the householder is present." he said, at the same time opening the doors of his van, lifting out a weighty looking bag of tools.

"If it's OK by you I'll get on then." he said again, disappearing quickly around the side of the house again.

"I'd jump on him if I had half a chance, he wouldn't be so polite if he knew what was going on in my mind right now." Donna said, grinning and using her key to open her front door.

Helping her friend to take off her coat she asked if she wanted a drink, Lisa nodded asking for he usual Vodka and lemonade.

Donna- Marie disappeared into the kitchen, Lisa was full of praise for the way she kept the house in such a pristine condition, especially since she had been alone for over two years now, Oliver her partner, had walked out on her, after three years …no reason given! Luckily though, there weren't any children.

Her friend came back carrying a tray in her hand, and ambled slowly over to the drinks cabinet, to prepare the drinks,

Handing Lisa her drink she switched on the TV hoping to see her usual Australian soap, but football had taken precedence.

Flicking through the programmes she finally let it settle on the Tele-text page, then sat down opposite her friend, who had already slipped of her shoes and folded her legs beneath her, on the settee

After a while Lisa felt a little uncomfortable, becoming aware that her friend was staring at her, her large brown eyes scrutinising her every movement, not saying anything.

"What's up? Is this some kind of silent inquisition or something" Lisa asked.

"Well darling don't think I'm probing, but we have got to know each other quite well these last few weeks, more than we did in all the years we've known each other in fact, but there's something spooking me... something I don't truly understand." Donna said.

"About today you mean?" Lisa asked.

"No, not just today, any day, I've never seen you show such hate to anyone, like the venom you show to Marks, I know you told me why before, but it seems to me there has to be more to it… that's all." Donna explained.

A long silence prevailed, the only distraction being the hum of the half muted music coming from the television screen, flashing the different colour texts.

"The bastard raped me! Christmas eve, a month before Martyn and I were married," Lisa mumbled, her voice hardly audible.

"Can you pass that by me again." Donna said, not really believing what she had just heard.

Lisa repeated her shocking revelation.

Donna placed her drink on the coffee table, and then jumped up quickly, putting her arms around her friend, cradling her head on her breast. Remaining silent.

"I wanted to tell you the last time we spoke but I felt so ashamed, I keep on thinking it was my fault, he seemed so much a man of the world, I couldn't help flirting with him, you know what it's like when you're young."

"Don't utter another word darling I can see and feel the hurt you're suffering, don't put yourself through it again. I think I understand now, you're right… he truly is a swine from hell"

Donna hugged and consoled her sobbing friend for what seemed an eternity.

"Perhaps going away is the only solution," she suggested, quietly.

"Maybe it is… but I can't think straight right now, there's just too much on my mind," Lisa said, in between her erratic sobs.

Donna went to retrieve their coats, offering to drive them to her home, she agreed and made to switch the television off, and as she did, she caught sight of some back numbers from the lottery results, up on the screen. Some of them looked familiar.

There were three of the family's birthday numbers there. Normally she would have been excited by now, even with the ten-pound prize. But recalled Martyn had always kept the tickets, and dismissed it all as irrelevant.

Turning away from her fanciful thoughts, she jumped into the car, and tried to think about all the mundane tasks she had to perform, in her effort to try and make home life, normal for the kids again.

Kirsty had changed since being away, she had become quite the little woman, growing up very quickly. Becoming thoughtful now, volunteering errands, even filling in the slack time with Ben. A real help around the house. Lisa mused.

She was like Martyn in so many ways, even the way she looked. Her deep blue eyes, the dimple on her chin, and her long loose blonde hair. What's more she seemed to revel in responsibility, needing no excuse to take the lead in awkward situations, even at this tender age.

Toni and Bill had brought them back from Plymouth late yesterday morning, but they didn't stay long themselves.

Lisa wished she had seen more of her sister over the years. They had never been very close, like some sisters she knew.

Toni was seven years older than her, and had married Bill, a sailor in the merchant marine. She had left home when Lisa was in her early teens, never really there when she needed advice in her formative years, but both Bill and Toni had been angels these past weeks... the salt of the earth. Suddenly she saw her sister in a different light, knowing now, that she'd be forever in her debt.

Lisa decided to stay home with the children for another week, to try and get them used to a routine without Martyn, but Ben was already asking for his Daddy.

She decided to take the children for a walk down to the little shopping centre on the edge of the estate to collect the Sunday papers. It was something that Martyn always used to do, always buying the financial times to check how the markets were performing, especially if he'd been away on business.

Later that day, while preparing lunch, Kirsty had switched the television on, and it got her wondering how many birthday numbers had actually come up, after catching sight of those lucky numbers at Donna's. She made a mental note to check them out.

After lunch, while Kirsty was phoning her friend, she switched the TV on again...

Martyn had always done a fixed line, filling in the ticket with the family's birth dates. He had always done the same thing week on week. It had become a kind of family ritual. Occasionally he would try his luck with a lucky dip, but would never miss their birth dates.

She remembered telling him at the time the lottery had first started, that she didn't think birthdays were a good idea, as they never went past thirty one, leaving out the forties altogether. Not very good for someone born late in the month, but he always insisted on doing it his way, bragging he'd scoop up the big prize one day.

Pen at the ready, she jotted down the numbers from the Saturday draw, that fateful week, a fortnight ago, she soon realised there were more than three, there was five, then ...six!

By the time she had crossed them off, her heart raced, thumping with excitement, she couldn't believe it at first, but realised all the birthdates tallied.

That's what must have caught her eye over at Donna's house. She thought.

Twenty-one, Martyn's birthdate, Twenty-nine...her's, Sixteen.. Kirty's, Ben's the thirtieth, Martyn's mother the ninth, with Lisa's father, Eric's August birthday, bagging the bonus... number thirteen.

She checked again and again, but still took a long time for the fact to sink in.

'My God! He did crack it then, always saying he would, she muttered, as if talking to herself.

Kirsty, noticing her Mother's mounting excitement, asked.

"What's the matter Mummy?"

Calming down a little and realising that she was probably building up false hopes, saying.

"Oh! it doesn't matter darling it's something and nothing really," she said, suddenly resigned to the fact that there wouldn't be a ticket anyway. In all probability, there never would be one, suddenly aware that she had probably upset her daughter. Changing her train of thought, she vowed not to promote anymore emotional high's and low's. It was becoming much too upsetting.

It wasn't until she had got the children off to bed that curiosity nagged at her yet again. She just had to confirm that it wasn't just a dream, had to view the numbers one more time.

Switching on the TV, she checked again... "Oh! God it's true... it's true," she mouthed, out aloud.

Aware that all these expectations could add to her grief, especially if there was no ticket. Yet it continued to haunt her, and try as may, she couldn't stop thinking about it.

Later, while in bed, she lay awake and wondered about the events that had surrounding her, since Martyn's demise. She realised now, of course, that he had met his end dressed in his prop clothes outfit.

The blazer, which he had left for work in, had been found, and returned by Jeremy....

She hadn't connected it at that time, what with being screwed up emotionally with that floozy of his, and later, of course, she was to have him buried him in that same outfit.

She clearly recalled cleaning out his pockets on a number of occasions in the past, in order to send it for dry cleaning, and clearly remembered that she had discovered an old crumpled ticket then.

Martyn had a habit of squashing them into a little pocket, sewn into his larger inside one. Could it be there now? She wondered.

But if her memory was serving her right, she had searched through all his pockets, around the time of his funeral and found nothing.

Yet the thought still haunted her. What if she had searched the wrong pocket, or had simply forgotten to feel around in the little pocket.

Before getting off to sleep she resolved to call in at Desmond News agents, to find out once and for all if Martyn had bought a ticket that week. There was always the possibility that he hadn't, then all this speculation would be for nothing.

If, on the other hand, she found out that he'd purchased one... Well... she'd cross that bridge when she came to it. Turning around on to her side, she tried hard to switch off from a myriad of thoughts, invading her, in the cold lonely bed.

The following morning she took the children to the town's memorial park, it was cold and she wasn't really in the mood, but it was fatal to promise the kids anything, they would nag her until she capitulated, especially little Ben.

Determined not to ask Donna for her car again she had decided to travel by bus.

Anyway, the kids loved travelling that way, but for her it meant waiting at that draughty bus stop, invariably meeting well meaning neighbours, offering up their mind numbing sympathy again.

As they waited at the stop, a black BMW came to a halt, then reversed until stopping alongside her and the children, from the shadow a suave, good looking moustachioed man came into view, leaning over to the passenger side, addressing her through the open window.

It was her bogey-man Marks.

"Are you off up to town?" he asked.

"No!" Lisa replied, "We are not going as far as that, we're going over to the railway station, travelling down to Plymouth to see my sister, she lied, saying the first thing that came to mind.

"Oh!" Marks exclaimed, his facial expression soured with disappointment.

"Well I'd like to see you when you come back then, there's lots of loose ends to tie up with the business, Oh! And incidentally, Carrol asked me to tell you that she'd like to see you. You know where she lives now, don't you." he said.

"Yes, but you'd better tell her we won't be back for some time." Lisa said, relieved to see the bus for Penington pull up behind his car.

"OK! I'll do that. Bye then, I'll see you when you get back." he shouted, pulling off slowly, the electric window snapping back into place, neatly ending their conversation.

While on the bus, Kirsty asked her why she had said they were going to Plymouth.

"I can't tell you the reason right now Darling, but what Mummy just did was to tell a white lie, it's not as serious as a deliberate one, but there was a good reason for it.

One day I'll tell you all about it," Lisa replied.

Braving the chilly autumn air, Lisa enjoyed watching the children's playful antics.

She joined in the fun with them, running alongside them and pushing them on the swings, it was a welcome break from the sombre atmosphere at home. But she knew she couldn't put the real world off for long, she had to check out the newsagents, and find out whether Martyn had bought a ticket or not.

Not wanting to make her enquiries too obvious, she dropped the kids off with Donna, at Bric-a-Brac, their shop, on Hillingdon road, just off the high street.

Doing things this way, would obviously give her more time to think about how she could ask her questions, without arousing too much suspicion.

When she finally arrived at the newsagents in the centre of the busy town, she was relieved to find that the man Roly wasn't there, she knew him by sight, and it had occurred to her, that perhaps, unbeknown to her, he'd been at the funeral, and would recognise her.

Pleased that the woman about to serve her was a stranger, she requested a news paper and a pack of cigarettes, casually mentioning she had just spotted that man's poor wife in the high street, the one who had been killed in that motor accident up at Beakers Grove a few weeks ago.

It seemed to do the trick, the woman suddenly became very talkative.

"Yes, Michael...Whittle, or something... my husband knew him, sold him a lottery ticket the very day he was killed, saw him every week in fact. Good customer of ours, came in every Friday evening, always had a joke and a laugh.... left two children I believe...sad isn't it." she said, handing Lisa the pack of cigarettes, before beginning to elaborate,

" My Roly was saying how ironical it would be, if his had been the winning ticket. We know from the organisers that the other half of the eight million jackpot hasn't been claimed yet, and they know it came from a terminal somewhere here in Penington,"

Lisa was relieved to exit the shop, the feelings of excitement bubbling up inside her. Thinking hard about what the woman said, it was confirmation really that the winner was local, so there was a good chance it was Martyn's ticket after all...but where was the elusive ticket?

Up until this moment she had enjoyed checking events out, mainly because it gave her a sense of purpose. Now though, she knew she'd have to follow it all through, take matters a lot more seriously. The excitement had the effect of making her feel alive again, There was hope now. Something left to strive for. She knew she was going to explore every avenue of possibility from that moment on.

But what about the shady lady Nicol?. could he have left the ticket with her, perhaps it was still in her flat and she had no knowledge about it. She had to check that out first.

She decided not to mention anything to anybody, not even her friend...she was aware that her biggest problem would be getting into Nicol's apartment without any real help,

It was either that, or she'd have to find someone, completely unconnected, to assist her.

Whatever happened, she knew she would have to wait until the kids started back at their schools on Monday.

Returning to Bric-a-Brac, she collected the kids and returned home by bus, racking her brains, trying hard to think of someone who could fit the bill to help her.

Quite suddenly she realised, the answer was staring her right in the face.

Zac...Zac Tinsley, her step brother, he was the obvious choice... the black sheep in fact, he had always been in and out of prison, had only just been released in fact, after serving eighteen months for burglary.

She had never had much to do with him, he was Barbara's son, so there wasn't even a blood link, but she had always classed him as her step- brother, even though he wasn't really.

He hadn't attended the funeral, but she knew he had got on well with Martyn, striking up quite a friendship with him after a family wedding a few years back, and had come down to visit them a couple of times since.

Picking up the phone she asked for Eric, but the voice on the other end seemed strange to her, until he said his name was Zac. Lisa couldn't believe her luck, she had hoped she could have got in touch with him via Eric or Bab's.

He told her that her Dad and Barbara had just gone out, then commiserated with her about her loss and apologised for not attending the funeral, asking if he could pass on a message.

"It's just that I have a leaky header tank, water is seeping through the ceiling into Kirsty's bedroom, and I've got a back door that jams every time I close it, Eric told me at the funeral if there was anything I needed doing...to call him.

I'd pay for the work of course," she intimated

"Well as it happens I'm idle at the moment, you probably heard that I've just got out again, I've been a guest of her majesty's government, and I'm looking to be gainfully employed. I could come down for a couple of days if you want, what d'you say?" he suggested.

"That would be brilliant, could you make it Monday next?" Lisa asked.

"Yeh! I've got nothing else to do, I could be there about mid morning, is that alright with you?" he proposed.

"That would be great I'll see you then, it'll be nice to see you again Bro. Oh! and give my best to Eric and Barbara, tell them I'll make an effort to come up and see them sometime... Cheerio Zac, see you Monday then." she said, replacing the receiver.

True to his word Zac arrived around eleven thirty, pulling up outside the house in an ancient white Transit van. A thick set young man of average height, with wispy black thinning hair, receding at the temples, sporting a earring in his right ear, and a thick gold chain around his neck, that glinted above his open collar.

He looked older than his twenty three years, as he sauntered up to the front door with a couple of wood saws tucked under one arm, and carrying a carpenter's holdall full of tools in the other.

She opened the door to him,

"You've come well equipped by the look of that bag," she said, by way of greeting.

"Yeah, it's all here, every thing we need Sis, get the kettle on then, and you can show me what you are wanting done." he replied.

She directed him to a chair at the table in the kitchen.

Filling up the kettle she wondered how he'd take it when she broached the real meaning of why she needed his services.

"Good journey down?" she asked.

"Alright after I got off that manic motorway, couldn't get out of the slow lane with that junk van of mine, it won't do more than forty... engine needs a re-bore really." he replied, sounding serious now.

"How are things now Lisa? have you got over the shock of it all yet."

"I don't think I ever will, to be honest Zac, nothing seems to be going right, my problems seem to be mounting one upon another, to tell you the truth I'm a bit scared about how you'll re-act when you realise I've got you down here under false pretences,"

"What you mean? I don't understand," Zac asked.

"Well, to tell you the honest truth. It's nothing to do with odd jobs really, but saying that. I really have got a door that sticks. No, it's to do with what happened to Martyn, some unfinished business that has left a bad taste in my mouth, I don't know if you know it or not, but he was killed after leaving his fancy woman that night," she blurted.

"No! I didn't know…I knew about the accident of course, you mean he was playing away from home. Well that really surprises me, I had him figured as a regular sort of fella, and I thought you two were a real item. You both seemed so happy before.

Well nothing's what it seems…is it? It seems everything is sent to try us I suppose. What's the real problem then Sis?" he asked.

"Well I have to get into that woman's flat somehow, I want to retrieve some things that are important to me, letters, trinkets that he gave her, I don't want that bitch to have a single thing that belonged to Martyn," she said, vindictively.

"I can understand that, I know where you're coming from, but how can you think so much of him now when you say he had a mistress. Most women I know would have killed him them selves, for doing the dirty like he done to you," he said.

"It was my fault really, giving him all those ultimatums about his life…he loved acting, been a member of the amateur dramatic club since not long after leaving school, he wouldn't give it up, he'd give me up first… I suppose that's what he did really; you could say I drove him into that bitch's arms. If it hadn't been her it would have been someone else." she explained.

"There's no violence involved in this is there? I can't take that chance, I'm out on parole as it is." he asked.

No! Nothing like that, I just want to get his things back… that's all," she said.

"OK! But I will still need paying when the job is done, I need the money- when do you plan to start?" he probed.

"As soon as you are ready to, I expect you'll want to take a look at the place she lives first, the only thing I know for certain is that she has a job, works through the day, so it would have to be sometime when she's out of the flat," Lisa suggested.

"OK! As soon as I've finished my coffee we'll get down there and take a shufty." Zac said, sounding very authoritative.

CHAPTER 4

Zac parked the van up at the Centre Grove multi story, near the town centre, he didn't want any complications, if for any reason, if they were caught in Nicol's flat.

They walked half the length of Penington high street to Llanion's florist shop, and he ushered Lisa inside, then taking in the scene, he rolled his eyes, indicating a door down at the other side of the room, opposite a shelf of ornate vases, containing dried flowers.

It was an entrance he had found out about when reconnoitring the area, leading up to the apartments upstairs.

Pretending to examine a vase he stepped back and shadowed Lisa at the door with his large frame, panning his eyes around again, he made sure the shop assistant wasn't looking, and then quickly gave Lisa a nod to go.

She turned the key that was already in the lock and exited, closing the door quietly behind her.

She found herself in the middle of a passageway. To the right of her was the side entrance door, and opposite the staircase, which lead up to the flats on the second landing.

Creeping carefully upstairs, she got on to the landing, then moved on a little further to the second apartment door, and waited, listening for tell tale signs of occupancy.

Hearing nothing, she went down stairs again, and hovered around the front door waiting for a shadow to materialise through the opaque glass.

Seconds later Zac approached, she opened the door to him and followed him up the stairs as he fiddled with an assorted bunch of key probes, on a large fob ring.

He soon triggered the single barrel mechanism, opening the door in an instant.

"Do you want me to search with you?" he asked.

"Yes if you would, look for letters and stuff, but in particular, a pendant... attached to a gold chain." Lisa said, knowing that she had to lie to him again. There wasn't a pendant, but it was too risky at this stage, to let him know what she was really looking for.

Lisa came across a small parcel of letters tied up with string. Flicking quickly through them, she came across one with Martyn's unmistakable handwriting. Opening it, she scanned through the first few of lines a number of times, then surprised herself by not wanting to read anymore.

She knew in her heart that Martyn loved her, the only conflict was, which one had he really loved, her, or his damned acting career. The bitch Nicol, hadn't even come into the frame as far as she was concerned… she was just an assessory.

Zac appeared from the bedroom holding up a handful of jewellery.

"There's all kinds of trinkets here, except that pendant you described… what do you want me to do with it all?" he asked.

" Well that's up to you… but on your head be it, I've got the letters, I wouldn't be at all surprised if she's already sold the pendant, that would be her style, what you say to having one more quick look around, then we'll call it a day. Oh! and by the way little brother, don't take anything too valuable, we don't want your friends the old bill nosing around, do we?" she warned.

They put everything back the way they found it, Lisa was reasonably satisfied by now that the ticket wasn't there, there was a minute chance that Nicol had found it, she thought, but if she had, everyone in the world would have known it by now.

They made a swift exit from the apartments by way of the side door, and collected the van from the multi-storey.

On arriving home, she knew she would have ask Zac to do her another favour.

Donna had taken Ben to his new nursery school at Penington that morning, leaving her just a half an hour before she was due to pick him up.

"Could you drive me?" she asked.

"I could, but I won't… I've got to see the racing on channel four, I've put a bet on just about every horse in the race." He said, smirking.

"Well can I borrow the van then? Lisa asked.

"OK, but I hope you can handle the crate properly, it's only insured for one, so on your head be it." he replied.

For a moment there, she was reminded of Martyn' macho moments, it seemed to her that most men are tarred with the same brush... innate selfishness!

She took the short cut through Beakers Grove, travelling the same road where Martyn had met his fate. After the accident she had vowed never to go that way again, but a weird feeling inside her, drove her on.

Slowing down at the farm gate, opposite the grass verge where the accident had occurred, she felt her whole body shiver, as she brought the car to a halt further on down the road.

Exiting the van, she took a few tentative steps around the rear of it to survey the scene, as she walked on slowly in the direction of the green, she could plainly see the skid marks still visible for a hundred yards or so, on the side of the narrow country road.

Crying now, she collapsed onto her knees in the long damp grass, and found herself repeating Martyn's name over and over again, eventually toppling over and ending up face downwards like someone in prayer, beating her fists upon the singed grass, as she wept profusely...

"I promise you...I promise you my darling, I 'll find out the truth and we shall have our revenge..."

At the nursery, the pretty young carer Allison Dears met her as soon as she entered the play area. She was late, and Ben was the only child left there.

"I'm sorry I'm not on time but it couldn't be helped... how's he been, has he been good boy?" she asked, lifting Ben from the carer's out stretched arms.

"Surprisingly good really...most kids cry the house down on their first day but he seems to have enjoyed every minute of it." Allison explained.

Lisa promised she would be on time the following day, and bid her goodbyes before strapping her sleepy son into the portable child's seat, Zac had fixed up in between the driver and passenger seat at the front of the van.

Glancing down repeatedly at her son on the journey home, a wave of rage and anger began to wash all over her yet again. The rage seemed insurmountable.

'Martyn you damned idiot… why did you let him ruin our lives.' she said, reaching over, gently brushing her little son's angelic face,

' Don't worry I'll make him pay… Oh yes, we will make him pay, won't we my little one.'

Suddenly, becoming aware her anger was become self-destructive, she tried hard to recall something her friend had once said.

'If you could turn the tables… take the lead, then you'd be the hunter, and him the hunted' She would remember this advice, and use it as a kind of mantra for the future.

When she finally arrived home, her brother took the wheel and drove her down to pick Kirsty up from the Forest Park Primary school. Happy, at last, that he had placed his bets at the Kempton race meeting

Later that day, after tea, Zac played hide and seek with the kids for best part of the evening. They both obviously loved their new- found uncle, causing Lisa all sorts of trouble, trying to get them to bed for the night.

Ben insisted that his new friend tell him a bedtime story, before taking his hand and leading him upstairs.

While he was occupied Lisa tried to work out how best he could help her with her last option, she wondered what his reaction would be when she asked for help in her grizzly task. How would he react? Helping her to break into the apartment was one thing, but asking him to disturb her husband's grave, was a bit ghoulish, to say the least.

Perhaps he would have some religious or ethical objection, just because he'd been in prison didn't automatically mean he was devoid of feelings or convictions.

He could say yeah, or nay of course, but if by chance he did agree, she would have to keep him from knowing what her main purpose was. Retrieving the ticket. If there was one… that is!

Later Zac came trouncing down stairs, with a great smirk growing across his face.

"That kid of yours is real smart ass, d'you know what he did, he pretended to fall asleep when I was reading the story...you know like a dog with one eye open, and every time I tried to creep away, the little devil called me back, making me read it all over again. Not bad for three and a quarter eh!." he said, still grinning.

"You're really good with kids Zac, it's a wonder some woman hasn't snapped you up before now." Lisa said, adding, "Do you fancy a drink?"

Zac nodded.

"What's your poison?' she queried.

"Scotch on the rocks...if you have it." he replied.

"I've got whiskey, but no ice... will water do?" she quizzed.

He nodded in the affirmative again.

Handing her brother the drink, she found herself blurting;

"Look, I don't quite know how to say this, but I want you to help me again, this time though, I'd understand if you refused, It's totally against the law, but I can't think of anybody else who could help me with this."

"What's this? then Sis? The way you are talking, it sounds as if you want to hire a hit-man or something." Zac said, with a puzzled look growing across his face.

"Well it's not as bad as that, its been done before, but if we are caught, we would probably end up as guests of her majesty." she said.

OK! You've got my attention woman, what is it?" he probed.

"I want you to open up Martyn's grave," she said, in a voice that was hardly audible.

"Beg your pardon." was all Zac could think to say.

"I have to get into my husband's grave somehow," she repeated again.

"Good God… what the hell for woman?" he asked, looking gob smacked.

"Well…it's the ring you see…her wedding ring. I want it, like the letters, I want everything that belongs to me, do you understand?" she said.

"Yeh! I think I do, but it seems a hell of a lot of trouble to go to just for a ring." he spat back.

"Look it means everything to me, don't you see I blame myself for Martyn's death...that ring should have been the embodiment of our love," she explained.

"Surely though you must have known the ring was to be buried with him," he said.

"Our ring yes, but not that bitch's. When I had it out with her, she told me he was wearing her ring... and had discarded mine," Lisa said, keeping her explanation as close to what Nicol had said, hoping to ward off any further curiosity on his part.

" Oh! I see, now I think I understand, that puts a different complexion on it, I can see that's very important to you, being a woman 'an all..." there was a long silence before he spoke again.

"OK then I'll do it, but what's in it for me, and when do you plan to get started on this ghoulish adventure?"

"The answer to the first part of your question is nothing...but if things turn out like I've planned... everything! And lot's of it, I can't tell you anymore than that right now. But you could say it's something like an insurance policy... of sorts. The second part of your question is, as soon as you are ready." she said, feeling uneasy about having to lie again, but at least there was some truth in her explanation.

She had never acted this way before, but there was too much at stake. She had no choice. Her family's future depended on it.

"Before you pour me another drink I think you ought to show me where this cemetery is especially now the kids are safely tucked up, is it very far?" he probed.

"It's the Penington Municipal cemetery, about ten minutes away, half an hour and we should be there and back, I could ask Pam next door to keep an eye on the kids..."she suggested.

"No! don't do that, we don't want attract any attention, the kids will be alright. Don't worry we'll be back in no time at all, I just got to see where it is and find out what sort of tools we'll need to do the job." Zac said.

Lisa went upstairs to check if the children were asleep, she had let Ben sleep with Kirsty since they had come back from Toni's, hoping it would help take their minds off the situation in the house.

When they arrived at the cemetery, the high, ornate Victorian gates were chained and padlocked in two places. Zac asked her to point out roughly where the grave was, Lisa indicated a place up ahead, about twenty metres to the right from the main gates, reminding him there was no grave stone yet.

He ordered her to stay put in the van while he reconnoitred the area.

She watched him as he walked toward the entrance, then veering off to the right; he quickly disappeared out of view.

Ten minutes or so later, he was back, breathing heavily,

"I had to jump the railings, for what I can see there's only one snag, the road light! It illuminates the whole area, but that could be a good thing, the grave itself is one row removed from the edge of the walkway," he said.

"Yes, but surely no one walks around there at night." Lisa cut in.

"You'd be surprised, I've had some of my best romantic moments in places like that," Zac said, adding,

"No seriously, we'll have to rig some kind of tent up, something that I'll be able to stand up in. A dark coloured one preferably, something that doesn't stand out too much when I erect it over the plot. Oh and we'll need a couple of those camping lamps so if anyone did came through that way, they'd think it was grave being dug by day and left over night,"

Lisa put her head in to her hands, and began to sob,

"I don't think I can do it, not in a tent.... that near to Martyn."

"Don't worry Sis, I'll do the spadework, you can stay in the van until the job is done, you'd only have to come over to get the ring, and I could do that if you want." he said.

"No! I have to steel up some courage and see him one more time, we didn't even have a chance to say goodbye." she cried.

Tomorrow night then, assuming it's dry and overcast... is that OK with you? We'll go into town tomorrow and buy the tent and stuff."

Lisa didn't say anymore, remaining mute all the way back home.

The following morning Lisa knocked on Zac's bedroom door telling him she was using the van to take the children to school, and reminded about their shopping trip.

Zac grunted and pulled the sheet over his head, hoping to get back off to sleep again. But he knew he wouldn't.

There was a thousand and one things swirling around in his mind, not least the job he'd promised to do, he had done a lot of dodgy things in his comparatively short life, but nothing so odd and spooky as this.

He had deliberately made out he was strong and unemotional to his step sister, but deep down inside him there was a well of squeamishness he hadn't confronted before. The questions were legion, what would his reaction be when he finally lifted the lid? Would he be haunted by it for the rest of his life?

The thought gave birth to the mechanics of it all, there was bound to be some kind of a whiff, he'd have to get a spray and face masks, he wouldn't let on to Lisa, of course.

Like most things in life, it had all been done before, it wouldn't be the first time someone had done this, or the last...no! He'd treat it as a one off; anyway, he could avoid looking if he wanted.

One thing though, it would be their secret, his and Lisa's, he could never breath a word of it to Eric or Barbara, or they'd think they were into some of devil worship or something.

Casting off the Duvet he ambled down stairs and walked into a closet, mistaking it for the kitchen. He still didn't know the layout of the house, but eventually found the right area, rummaging through the wall cupboards searching for something to eat. Choosing some Muesli, he drowned the concoction with milk that had been left on the table, and then switching on the radio he munched the serial, dressed in a pair of his late brother in law's pyjamas.

He was still dressed this way when Lisa arrived back home some time later,

"You've been a time, where have you been then?" he asked.

"I called in to see Donna, my partner at the shop, told her about you being here, explained you were doing some odd jobs for me." Lisa explained.

"That's your friend you were telling me about is it?" he probed again.

"Yes she wanted to come around tonight to meet you, but I put her off, told her we were taking the kids out for a cinema treat in Penington." she explained.

"Good." Zac said, getting up at last from the sofa.

Lisa caught sight of the pyjamas, taken aback, her first thoughts were to rip into him, she'd completely forgotten she had loaned them to him, when he'd first arrived.

"I see you had your breakfast then...typical, don't men ever tidy up after them," she said, placing the crockery into the washing up bowl.

"What time are you planning on going in to town?" she enquired.

"In about half an hour or so, I'll go and get dressed OK." he said, disappearing upstairs.

Lisa wondered if Pam next door would look after the kids again, otherwise it would mean them over to Donna's Maries house and that would surely generate a new agenda of questions. Luckily Pam agreed once again.

They arrived into town just before noon. Zac wasn't enjoying the shopping trip at all, as they had walked the length of the high street twice, and still hadn't found the goods they needed. He was lugging a small mandrel spade and camping lamp, but still needed a dark coloured tent, something he would be able to stand up in to complete his grizzly task.

They both agreed that some refreshment was on the cards, and called in at the Corner Café. And as soon as they entered, Lisa spotted Donna sitting up at the top end of the room, in conversation with someone she didn't know. Instinctively, she thought she should get back out to the street again, but realised that would be too obvious.

Relieved her friend hadn't spotted them, she deliberately sat with her back to her.

"Do you fancy something to eat?" Zac asked

No, I'm not really hungry, you order if you want." she said, hoping he wouldn't complicate matters by meeting her friend.

Her intuition telling her she would be attracted to him, being footloose these days. It didn't take much imagination to realise that he'd probably tell her everything, if they began some form of a relationship. And that in turn would surely complicate matters again, evolving into yet another question and answer time.

No! All she needed was Zac's help, with the hope that he'd go back home eventually, and forget all about it.

But it wasn't to be, her friend spotted her, tapping her on the shoulder,

"So this is your little secret… is it, your own DIY man, and in the family too." Donna said, playfully.

Lisa smiled an introduced her stepbrother.

Spotting the spade and other implements, she commented

"Oh he's a gardener too, you can come to my place any time my man, I've got a hundred and one jobs to attend to." she said, smiling down at Zac.

"Just give me the word," he said.

After reporting the state of play at the shop she glanced at her watch saying she had better get back to Bric a Brac, and bid them goodbye, adding she was looking forward to meeting him properly the following night.

"She's dishy." Zac said, as soon as she had departed.

"Bit old for you." Lisa replied, sardonically.

"Don't worry I'm a lot older than I look Sis." He quipped.

They made several more forages up and down the high street, before Zac eventually found a tent…a military bivouac type, at the Army and navy store, before making their way home.

Kirsty and Ben seemed to think the tent had been bought for them, and soon had him erect it in the living room, playing games well into the evening.

Later she took them around to Pam's next door, always thankful that she had such a generous neighbour.

Lisa suggested that they take a flask of whiskey with them, it was already getting chilly, and Zac would need some kind of lift, even if it was one from a bottle.

"Right then, it's all set, I've put everything in the van…. what time have you got?" Zac asked.

"Ten thirty, how long do you think it will take?" she asked.

"How the devil do I know, I don't do this kind of thing for a living yer' know." he spat back.

"OK! Let's be off." he ordered.

On the way there the windscreen began to glisten with fine droplets of rain.

"That's all we need now, but at least the sky is overcast." he mumbled, flicking the wipers on.

As they turned into the car park Lisa pointed out a white transit van, parked up in the shadows near the far end of the empty car park.

"D'you think they have some sort of security man working here at night." she quizzed.

"I shouldn't think so, they'd probably have those mobile security people calling at intervals, but you never know...so keep your eyes wide open while I'm over there," he said.

They decided to stay put for a while in the van, and as it turned out it was lucky they did.

Two people passed at intervals by the main gates, walking their dogs. Zac waited a minute longer, and said,

"Right! I'm off. Don't forget if you see anyone suspicious, say your boyfriend has just nipped away answering the call of nature or something, I'll probably see you in about an hour or so...OK?."

Collecting up the equipment from the back of the van, he placed the rolled up tent under one arm, and carried the sacks and tools in a bin bag, with his other.

Lisa watched him until he veered off to the right, then he disappeared.

Zac got to the crossing place, threw the tools over the railings, before checking to see there was no one around then jumped over himself, making his way gingerly over to his brother- in- law's plot.

Never having been a deep thinking man, the closest he had come to thinking philosophically, was when he'd been alone in his prison cell, and it suddenly occurred to him, he'd better start by apologising to his brother- in- law for what he was about to do. Strangely, he felt a lot better, after performing the little ritual.

It was still threatening to rain as he unpacked the tent. It was a military one, room enough for two men, but tall enough to work in. The problem he had was the amount of soil he would have to dig out, so he had brought a half dozen, strong builders sacks with him, so he wouldn't have to keep opening the tent flap.

It took him ten minutes to erect the tent that straddled over the entire plot. The light from the street lamp at the main gate was such, that he could still see what he was about, but it would be a different matter when he closed the flap up, he'd need to use his battery lamp then.

He removed the wilted flowers and wreaths, placing them neatly on a grave behind him, and used the small mandrel to loosen the freshly laid topsoil to a depth of six inches, before shovelling it into the sacks.

It wasn't going to be easy, he thought, as he filled all the sacks to three quarters full, before humping them outside, making sure they were hidden behind a large, memorial vault. Luckily, everything seemed to be running like clockwork, but he began to realise that when he had got down to a foot or more he'd have to use the lamp, estimating he'd have to dig down to about five feet, or more.

Switching on the lamp inside the tent he moved quickly to the outside, before securing the flap, and inspected the tent for any tell-tale light. Noticing a slither of light shining through at one of the corners, he quickly placed a shovel full of earth there to block it out.

He carried on digging for well over an hour, beginning to sweat profusely as the work got more and more awkward. He had dug down to about three feet, and now it meant getting down into the grave proper. Filling up the sacks up individually, his knees, elbows and hands were soaked through with the damp clay like earth.

It was time for a respite; so he'd pay Lisa a visit, he mused.

As soon as he tapped the side window of the van, he knew he'd made a gigantic mistake, Lisa, startled, literally jumped up a foot into the air banging her head on the roof, screaming her head off.

Opening the door quickly he muffled her mouth with his grimy hands.

"It's me Zacarius." he said, repeating it a number of times, taking hold of her shoulders.

It took a good three minutes before she regained a measure of control.

"You idiot you scared me half to death." she said, her face sporting the mud marks he'd left, making her appear even more frightened.

"Aye and lucky the window was closed otherwise you would have woke up all of Penington." he retorted, trying to calm the situation.

"Do you want me to come over with you now?" she asked.

"No, not yet, I'm just about down to half way, I just come over to see if everything is all right… Has anything untoward happened here?" he quizzed.

"The van…the one in the corner over there, well it's gone, I had to sink right down in my seat. A scruffy looking man got out and took what, I think what you would term, as a leea, leaving the door open. I could see a woman looking somewhat dishevelled, but I don't think they noticed me though." she replied.

"Don't worry about them, they were obviously in a world of their own, they probably thought we we're doing the same as them. Right Sis, I'll be off again, next time I come across it should be ready, and I'll take you over then OK!…are you sure you are up to it?" he asked.

"Yes I'll be alright, I wish I'd made a flask of tea… give me a swig of that whiskey will you, I'm freezing, but don't worry about me, just get on with the job." Lisa said.

Arriving back at the dig, he soon commenced his back-breaking work again, and it wasn't long before his shovel made the tell-tale sound of metal hitting wood.

Rubbing the residue of earth away, he caught sight of some movement in front of him. Frightened out of his wits by this time, he eventually realised it was his reflection, staring out at him, from the silver nameplate, he had uncovered.

Suddenly, beneath the eerie silence… he froze again, hearing the distinct sound of something, or someone scratching outside the tent.

Whatever he had heard, had moved now to the opposite side of the tent. Keeping his body perfectly still, he raised his right arm up slowly; somehow managing to turn the lamp off, and with his left hand gently lifted the door flap.

It was a dog: A large spotted Dalmatian, with a long leather lead trailing from his collar. Almost immediately, a voice called from the distance.

"Sebastian! come here...come here....... you little....."

It was obviously someone's pet, which had escaped from his owner, dragging the lead along with him.

Why did he choose tonight of all nights to explore this patch, Zac mused.

The animal obviously knew something furtive going on, and he wasn't about to go away easily, leaving Zac to try and work out how he could appease him.

Bravely, he lifted the flap up as far as it would go, and said in a firm, quiet voice,

"Come on boy...come on now...come to Zac... there's a good boy,"

Suddenly! without any warning the dog snarled, then lunged at him, scoring a hit on the back of his hand, drawing blood.

Mindful of the nearness of its owner, he thwarted a scream, but toppled and lost his balance, falling headlong on to the casket, splitting the lid of the coffin into two halves.

" Oh! my God...I'm sorry Martyn...so sorry Martyn.... it's not my fault honest. It was that blasted dog!" he cried.

The distant anonymous voice of authority boomed out yet again. This time the excited animal bounded away, finally heeding his masters voice, but not before his lead had snagged around the tent ropes, collapsing the tent to the ground.

Zac dragged himself painfully up on to his knees, bruised and bleeding now, from the wound on his hand, he scrabbled around to find the tell tale lamp, before crawling out from under the tent, inspecting for damage,

There was no way he was going to make a move until he was sure the animal had gone on his way. Hearing nothing suspicious, he skirted around the surrounding tombstones, stopping at each one, to take a swigs from the whiskey flask, as he listened for any alien sounds. Satisfied, he went back to the plot and fished inside the bin liner for the jemmy, the aerosol and mask.

It took him a long time to get the tent into some order, but eventually, he descended down into the hole again, and slowly prised up the shattered lid. Fortunately now, there was only a need to prise the bottom half off, then putting the mask on, he sprayed the area with the aerosol.

Not wanting to look at anything closely, he kept his eyes half closed, covering everything with a couple of the sacks.

Jumping out of the hole, he was finally ready for Lisa. But he wasn't looking forward to this part, even less than opening the box. He prayed she'd be in a fit state to handle it.

Lifting up the two planks he'd noticed outside the gravedigger's hut, he kept a beady eye out for the dog, and placed them next to the railings.

Then went over to fetch his sister

"Is everything OK here?" he asked.

Lisa nodded, looking nervous.

The two of them walked quickly over to the fence. Zac positioned the planks on to the top of it, before taking hold of her hand he held her while she climbed up, before jumping over to the other side. Using the same procedure to descend to the other side, leading her down into the cemetery.

Lisa was shivering, but not all her shaking was because of the cold, she felt fearful but she knew she had to be brave, even if it meant acting like some unfeeling robot.

She consoled herself by thinking if everything went all right the reward would be great. Anyway, she knew that Martyn would want it for her and the kids.

Arriving at the graveside Zac whispered, I've covered the top half, you won't see anything really, do what you have to do quickly then I'll pull you up."

Half closing her eyes she dangled her legs over the hole, then squinting down, she saw that if she lowered herself carefully she'd be able to rest her feet on each side of the coffin.

Tackling the first step successfully, she knew now, she'd have to open her eyes, to find the pocket, and found herself mumbling,'

"Oh Lord, I'm so sorry Martyn, I love you, please forgive me, my darling.... you know I have to do this...It's for our Kirsty and Ben."

Keeping her eyes blinkered, she pulled upwards and focused on the blazer, lifting the lapel she felt inside the inside pocket, then felt around knowing there was a little ticket pocket inside the main pocket. Probing with her fingers she felt something small and damp, pulling it out, she quickly realised it was the elusive lottery ticket.

At that instant Zac called out, asking if she was all right.

"Yes, yes I'm OK," she replied, carefully folding the small piece of damp paper, and placed it into her pocket.

"Pull me up! For God's sake Zac pull me up!" she cried, trying hard not to look down.

"Did you get the ring?" he asked.

"I've got it." she said, showing him the one she'd kept at the ready in another pocket.

The both looked relieved as Zac led the way back to the car park.

As soon has he's deposited Lisa into the van he made his way back to the site, and began to work hard and fast, replacing the residue of loose soil, before re- placing the wreaths and wilting poses of flowers back at the head of the grave.

Looking down at his handiwork, he apologised to Martyn, and heaven and earth once again.

Satisfied, he rolled up the tent, bagged up the tools and walked over to join his stepsister over at the car park.

CHAPTER 5

It was well past three a.m. when they got back home and the lights were out next door, Pam had said if they hadn't got back by midnight she would bed the children down in her spare room. It was obviously much too late to collect them now. Lisa mused.

Zac looked like a wild looking ancient Briton just back off a raid on a Roman garrison, his face covered in streaky brown marks, and his sleeve ripped, covered with dried blood smearing his hand.

Lisa's reflection stared back in a odd way from the mirror too, she looked like some badly made up pantomime dame. Her short blonde hair damp and bedraggled, with the bottom half of her face a muddy brown colour with traces of tear tracts, from her eye down to her mouth.

But that didn't matter right now, she thought, itching to switch the television on to compare the back numbers against the selection on her ticket, it wasn't important that she had checked them a half dozen times before… this time she held the ticket in her fist, and that placed it squarely into the realms of possibility.

She glanced over to Zac, sitting on the kitchen worktop finishing of the contents of the flask, she wished he would make a move, take a shower, do something, but he seemed too exhausted to move, he hadn't uttered a single word since coming back.

"Thanks little brother, you don't know what you've done for me, I feel as if I can get on with life now, don't you think you ought to get a shower or something," she suggested, looking at him admiringly. Suddenly, the flask he'd been nursing, toppled over and bounced onto the stainless steel sink, creating a series of crashing cymbal like sounds.

Zac had literally fallen asleep, she rushed over to him and managed to hold him, propping him up as he started to keel over, his eyelids closed. Conjuring up hidden reserves of strength she managed to ease his big frame off the worktop, then guided him down, until he sank to the tiled floor, like a rag doll.

The poor man was absolutely exhausted, and out to the world.

Realising she couldn't lift or drag him anywhere, she grabbed a cushion from the lounge and placed it under his head, then collecting the throw- over from the sofa she managed to roll him on to half of it, and covered him with the other half, before bidding him goodnight.

Reaching into the pocket of her jeans she pulled out the crumpled ticket and crept out of the kitchen closing the door quietly behind her.

Checking the numbers on Tele-Text once again comparing them with the one's on her newly acquired ticket, she went upstairs to bed and wondered if it was all a dream.

Lying on her back with her eyes fixed to the ceiling she knew she wouldn't sleep, what with all the excitement she felt, so she tried hard to come to grips with the jackpot win… what was it Mrs Desmond had said?

Two winners…half of eight million! That was four mill… but she'd believe it when she saw it, she mused.

Been lucky so far though, she thought, no one knew anything except Zac, of course. And that was how she'd like to keep it.

There shall be a reward for him of course- an in-direct one… hopefully. And what about Donna, what should she tell her?

Perhaps it was better to cross those bridges when she came to them.

Glancing at the bedside clock it read a quarter past four, it would be light in an hour, so it was pointless just lying there. Getting out of bed, she ambled down the stair- well and headed for the drinks cabinet, pouring herself a Vodka and lemonade. Still tired, she sat down on the sofa- chair, sipping the drink until she finally dozed off.

It was twenty five past seven when she woke again. Discarding her husband's old anorak she had used to cover herself, she went into the kitchen to check on Zac.

He was lying face down on the tiled floor, his head buried into the cushion with arms akimbo, snoring and muttering, intermittent gibberish.

There was still time yet before going to collect the children, enough time, she hoped to wake him up and get him off upstairs for a shower before they came back.

Zac spent the best part of the day in bed, which meant Lisa had a free reign with his van, ferrying the kids to and fro their schools.

A couple of hours later, he informed her that he was off down to town to get a haircut.

Donna was due to visit that night, it was plainly obvious that he was getting spruced up just for that, he didn't care tuppence about his appearance normally.

Now was her opportunity to get in touch with Camelot.

Her heart thumped and hands shook as she picked up the phone and dialled the number to their main office at Tolpit Lane.

"I.think...well... I.know, I have a winning ticket, for the Saturday draw, three weeks ago," she stammered.

"Your name please?" the girl asked.

Lisa told her, then without a pause blurted out that she lived in the town of Penington.

"I was about to ask you that, the girl said.

"Would you read the numbers that are on the ticket please?" she instructed.

Lisa began to read them like a Bingo checker would.

"Twenty one, key of the door, one and six, sweet sixteen...thirteen, unlucky for..."

The curt voice at the other end cut in quickly.

"There's no need for that sort of description Mrs Whittle just the numbers please...."

Lisa read them off again, after which there was a short respite, when a man's voice addressed her.

"Mrs Whittle?"

'Yes." she replied.

"Can you confirm your home town again." he asked.

"I already told the girl, Penington."she replied.

"Thank you. well it certainly seems, if what you are saying is correct, you could well have a winning ticket" he said, clearing his throat before going on,

"I'm sure there is no need to remind you to keep your ticket safe, there are three options with regard to your ticket, firstly, you can send it on to us… registered post of course, or secondly, wait until one of our representatives meets you at a venue of your choice, thirdly, you could bring it to us personally at our main office.

Do you have any objections to any publicity?"

"Yes! a lot of them, I don't want any, on no account do I want anyone calling at my home address," she directed.

"Right, I see… we will be in touch with you again by phone of course, when we will arrange a venue of your choice," he said then adding,

"Oh! and incidentally please phone us, so we shan't cross any wires so to speak…is that alright with you Mrs Whittle?"

Before she could answer he went on.

"Oh! and ask for a Mr Ken Denton, would you please… Well Mrs Whittle, Bye for now, until tomorrow then.

As soon as she heard his receiver click on the end of the line she screamed out

"Yah…Ooooooh!." in unrestrained excitement

"I can't believe it, is that all there is to it? I've done it…."she cried, talking to herself aloud.

Glancing down at the ticket still in her hand, she folded it, and placed it in her credit card wallet, before stuffing it down inside her Bra.

Her friend arrived at seven thirty clutching a bottle of Chablis.

Zac, his hair styled and cropped, with a quiff hanging over his forehead, rushed to open the door to her.

"You look different than when I saw you yesterday." Donna said.

"Oh! I've just had a wash and brush up that's all." he lied.

Lisa could hear them talking from the dining room and couldn't help a wry smile, knowing he had given himself one of the biggest makeovers of all time, since arriving back from the hairdressers in Penington.

The children ran to her side tugging at her arm, Kirsty shouting excitedly,

"You're having dinner with us, aren't you Aunty Don, each of them grabbing a hand, before tugging her towards the dining room.

Donna Marie, a tall brunette had on a navy, collarless two piece, body hugging crimpolene suit, adorned with a large string of silver coloured imitation pearls, she looked gorgeous beneath the pink glow of the hall light.

Lisa, greeting her, looked stunning too, her natural long blonde hair swept back at the sides, wearing a low cut body hugging pale yellow dress, which accentuated her slim curvaceous figure.

This was the first time she had taken any care with her appearance since before the funeral.

She had prepared her speciality, pan-fried veal with mustard salad. A dish Martyn had raved about after his business trips to France, with her favourite sweet, Vanilla peaches and cream for dessert. All five of them sat around the circular dining room table tucking into the meal, everyone on their best behaviour, except the kids, who continually squabbled, stealing tit- bits from each other's plate.

After the banquet Kirsty commandeered Zac again. He knew he'd made a rod for his own back with the kids, but he loved acting the clown.

Donna helped Lisa clear things away to the kitchen. Alone at last, she questioned her friend,

"Has Marks tried to meet you yet?"

"Well if he has, I haven't seen him, I've been out a lot lately," she replied.

"Do you still feel the same about him... you know, that revenge bit?" Donna questioned again.

"Well I keep on asking myself why he's got this fixation with me- then I think sometimes the man is crazy, I've never encouraged him, so it's all bound to come to a head one day, but I have to consider the kids they've had enough grief in recent weeks to last them a lifetime... I just can't let them have anymore grief," Lisa replied.

"Why don't you go on the attack then… have a once and for all show down with him, go nuclear…scare him silly," her friend suggested.

"I'd love to, but I've got to behave normally in order to get some sort of financial settlement, … you know, get out of the mess gracefully." she replied.

Later, after Zac had got the children off to sleep he came down stairs looking absolutely banjaxed.

"It was you who started the ball rolling little brother, they'll never let you off the hook now." Lisa said knowingly, grinning as she poured out their respective drinks.

Donna sat next to Zac on the sofa, the long split in her skirt accentuating her long shapely legs. Becoming curious, she asked,

"Lisa tells me you've got a way with the kids, it's about time you settled down and made some of your own isn't it?"

"I'm not a settled kind of bloke, I expect Lisa has told you all about me by now." he ventured.

"Not a lot, she's mentioned you have had some trouble staying on the right side of the law, that's all," she said.

"Well that's an under- statement, I've been playing silly beggars with authority ever since I can remember, but after that last stretch I made up my mind that I didn't want to be banged up anymore, I suppose what I'm saying is that if you can't control the sea… you just have to learn how to swim in it," Zac pontificated.

"Have you tried to get a proper job?" Lisa asked.

"Many times." Zac said, sounding somewhat philosophical.

"But when I mention prison, it's like saying the last job I had was in a sewage farm, the only perks being whatever came through the pipes. They sympathise, then the cunning buggers smell everything I touch,"

"I can understand that," Donna said, adding, "We'd offer you something down at the shop, but there's not enough work for the two of us as it is,"

Lisa, who hadn't said a lot until then, cut in.

"Don't worry something will turn up you'll see, it usually does when you can't see no further than your nose."

Lisa could see her friend was quite taken with Zac, he seemed to have a street wise, old head upon his young shoulders.

Perhaps it was the life he had led. Come to think of it, she thought, he wasn't too put out with their ghoulish adventure at the cemetery... he hadn't done that before, had he? He was Jack the lad alright.

The evening seemed to fly and Lisa was glad when she had packed her friend off in a taxi. Zac had arranged for one earlier when it was obvious everyone was too under the weather to get behind the wheel. Anyway she had got tired and a little bored what with being sidetracked most of the evening.

The following morning Zac lolled around in the lounge studying the sports page of the paper as usual, she hoped he would go out place a bet or something, so she could phone that Denton chap at Camelot. She had decided the Red Lion hotel up on the common would be as good as place as any to meet their representatives.

"I've got a date with your friend tonight we're going out for a drink," he said, still eyeing the sports page.

"Have you indeed, you're a quick worker. What time are you going?" she asked, her earlier thoughts about them well and truly vindicated, about them becoming an item.

"Oh! 'bout six thirty thereabouts." he said.

Realising he was set to hang around the house until then she thought she'd use the extension phone in her bedroom, to arrange a date with the Lottery rep's at seven the same evening.

Arriving at the Red Lion, a red bricked, mock Tudor hotel at seven pm on the dot, Lisa was greeted by a middle-aged woman, in a smart formal grey suit, introducing herself as Mrs Jenny Haynes.

Offering her hand, the lady queried, "It is Mrs Whittle isn't it?"

Lisa nodded.

" I'm one of the lottery representatives, my associates Mr Denton and David Jessop are waiting for us inside," she said, at the same time turning on heel, adding.

"Follow me please."

Lisa followed her, through the sumptuous red- carpeted hallway, then through the second doorway on their right, entering a dark oak panelled dining room with a brightly lit, cheerful looking, three-corner bar up at the far end of the room.

A tall greying, distinguished looking man came over to them and promptly introduced himself, stating his name as Denton.

"I spoke to you on the phone." he said, then introduced his colleague David Jessop.

"Here are our credentials," he said, producing a large, leather folding wallet. His photograph endorsed upon it, above an official looking stamp, which read The National Lottery, Camelot, directly underneath his signature.

Mrs Haynes and D.J. did the same.

"As you can see we are the official National Lottery rep's and I can confirm the numbers you read out to our girl at the office were the correct one's for the Saturday draw of three weeks ago.

You say you live in the town of Penington, and we are aware that a winning ticket was issued from a terminal there, so would you now show us your ticket please,"

Lisa had folded it into four and placed it inside a locket she had around her neck. Holding the locket with her left hand, she snapped it apart with her right, then pulling it out she unfolded it and placed it on to the wine coloured, velvet tablecloth directly in front of them.

Denton scrutinised it a number of times then turned it over, smiling, he said,

"I dare say you've hidden this in a few places judging by the folds," then taking a closer look he commented that it wasn't signed. He took a pen out of his pocket and handed it to Lisa indicating where her signature should be written.

After Lisa had done this he turned to his male colleague and said,

D.J. inform Mrs Whittle on the value of the prize,"

The short bald man in a light plain grey suit picked up the pen took a table mat and wrote down the sum of ;-

FOUR MILLION....TWO HUNDRED THOUSAND POUNDS... AND SIXTY TWO PENCE.

Passing it over to Lisa he said,

"I've done this because most of the people we meet just cannot comprehend what a sum as large as this really means when it's written down in digits,"

As Lisa examined what he had written, a waiter in a short red jacket and large black dicky bow, came across to their table, asking if they wanted to order drinks.

Mrs Haynes and D.J. wanted tonic water, Denton a whisky and pep.

"What's your tipple Mrs Whittle?" he asked.

"Vodka lemonade and a touch of lime if you don't mind," she replied.

The waiter retreated and DJ picked up the threads of the conversation again, saying,

"Mrs Haynes here is one of our top financial advisors, you'll appreciate with such a large amount of money it's not just a case of giving you a bankers cheque for the said amount, you could have one if you so wished... but that would be madness. The interest alone on this sum would amount to well over five thousand pounds a week so obviously the capital sum must be invested, in fact your prize money already is, waiting to be unlocked, so to speak, for you the lucky winner."

All the talk was making her head spin, conscious of her more immediate needs she found herself blurting out,

"Can I have a loan? A sum of money released on account,"

"Oh! of course." the Jenny Haynes said. "We have a financial plan tailored to different people's needs, obviously we'll need to discuss this further with you, so I suggest you come to our main office in Tolpits Lane and we will work out a plan for you, do you agree?" she said, again.

Lisa nodded in the affirmative.

The waiter placed their drinks on the table, and Denton interjected,

"In the meantime I'm sure Mrs Haynes here can make you an advance, until then. How much do you think you need? Bearing in mind it will only be for a couple of days." Denton cut in.

Even though she was the main player in this drama she still didn't really believe it.

She felt frightened, to ask for too much.

"Ten thousand…is that OK?" she stammered.

Mrs Haynes took out her cheque book and scribbled out the sum across it, then handed over her pen requesting that she sign a receipt for the cheque and ticket, which was then endorsed by all three of them.

The following morning, having got Kirsty and Ben ready for school she thought she had better let her brother know she was borrowing his van again.

Ascending the stairs to her brother's bedroom, she rapped on the door several times, but received no answer, twisting the door handle she found it wasn't locked, so she peeped inside.

The beggar wasn't there, the bed hadn't even been disturbed. Good grief he's a fast worker, she thought, he'd only met Donna a day ago, and now it looks as if he's plonked his size eleven's under her table already.

It wasn't her job to moralise, they were both over twenty one…well, he's only just, she mused, as she strapped Ben in the front seat and Kirsty in the back, on a old bench seat Zac had made up for her.

Blocking out any further thoughts of them, she used her concentration to drive the children to their respective schools.

A short time later, on arriving back home there was still no sign of her little brother, so she made herself a coffee and reflected on her experience at the Red Lion, hoping she hadn't come across as too naïve. She couldn't think of much to say, she'd been gobsmacked by it all really, but the ten thousand would get her that badly needed car, Zac's van was really doing her head in.

Collecting the mail in the hall, she sat down again, and quickly discarded the pile of junk mail, before opening an official looking envelope.

It was from Mason the solicitor, requesting her to attend the office at her earliest convenience, she wondered if she could fix an appointment right away.

Everything was beginning to take on a sense of urgency, she needed to tie up the loose ends of her 'old' life, right away and start afresh. Having now, what most people can only dream of, a key, the where with all.

Dialling his number, the girl receptionist seemed pleased when she called, saying,

"Mrs Whittle, I'm glad you got in touch, Peter was hoping you would, he told me if you did, to ask you to attend the office at two sharp, is that alright with you?"

Lisa said that it was, and was about to ask her why this was, when the girl ended their brief conversation, adding curtly.

"We shall look forward to seeing you then."

As soon as she replaced the receiver, the doorbell chimed out. Thinking it was Zac, she rushed to door, but it was the smiling face of her neighbour Pam.

"I have a message for you," she said, reading from a small piece of paper.

"Someone named Zac phoned this morning, Claire took the message before she went to school, said he'd been trying to get in touch with you, but to tell you not to worry, 'cos he's OK, staying at Donna's. he said, adding he'd see you later in the day."

"I wondered where the beggar had got to," Lisa mumbled.

"Is that the young man who's been staying with you?" Pam probed.

"That's him, he's my long lost brother… step brother really, he's come down from Altringham to do a few DIY jobs me," Lisa explained.

"Oh that's alright then, I wondered who he was, he looked a bit rough to me, you can't be too careful these days…can you?" she said.

For some unknown reason, Lisa was bursting to tell Pam about her lottery win.

She needed to tell someone. It was the same kind of feeling she had experienced when she'd first fallen in love, she wanted to share her good news with everybody, and Pam had been an excellent friend and neighbour ever since she and Martyn had come to the lose. But she resisted the urge, knowing she couldn't handle another tidal wave of excitement, she had to keep calm, keep her feet on the ground. Anyway, everybody would find out soon enough.

"You won't come in have a coffee or something?" Lisa asked, knowing the answer was in the question. She never had, ever since she had moved to Hunters Close.

"No, if you don't mind I have a couple of important errands listed today, I'll probably see you later, Bye now love." she said, turning in the direction of her house.

Closing the door, she knew she had better get her skates on too! She had to get moving…get that new car.

She had hoped Zac could have helped her choose it, it would probably have to be a second hand model, so he could make sure she wasn't sold a ringer.

She decided to call on him, instead.

The heavens opened up as she drove left into Cashmere Avenue, the windscreen wiper on the passenger side had given up the ghost again, and she would happily abandon the van on the side of the road, here and now, if she could.

Donna's car wasn't there, it looked as if she had gone to work.

The shop! She'd completely forgotten about it. That was another obvious question mark. She would probably give it to her friend of course, but decided to wait until thing were sorted out later. It was just one of a hundred things she'd have to come to grips with before too very long.

Zac opened the door wearing a raincoat a half a dozen sizes to small for him, it was a vain attempt to mask the suit he was born in, it was obviously Donna's UPVC Mac, he was using as a dressing gown substitute.

"Hi! Sis, Donna has gone to the shop, come on in." he said.

"You don't let the grass grow under your feet do you little brother, are you two an item already?" Lisa questioned.

"Well lets just say we are heading that way, came back a bit late last night then had a few more drinks here, neither of us could drive so I requested permission to stay…and it worked too," he explained.

"No need to ask where you slept then," she said, knowingly.

"No need at all." Zac replied.

"Look, I haven't come round to nose around, the real reason I'm here is to ask you to help me choose a car, that van of yours is driving me potty." Lisa said.

"You mean you are actually going to give it back to me." he said, grinning.

"You're more than welcome to it, I've seen a few cars I fancy down at Corner Park Motors, do you think you could find some time to run me over there? give them the once over," she asked.

"Of course I can, need a shave first though, hang on in there, make yourself some coffee or something, I won't be a jiff." he said, disappearing into the bathroom.

Fifteen minutes later, and they were on their way.

"Have you told the kids you are getting a new car?" Zac asked.

"No I want to surprise them when I pick them up," Lisa explained.

"What sort of price range are you looking at?" he asked again.

"Something in between five to six thousand I thought," she replied.

"Got anything in mind?" he questioned, again.

"I'd like a mini, you know, the same as I had before, but I think the kids want something bigger, especially Kirsty," she answered, already getting fed up with the inquisition.

The rain was falling even heavier when they arrived at the garage, and the pair of them spent a cold wet hour searching around the sprawling motor mart looking at all sorts of vehicles from the ordinary to the exotic.

Lisa finally plumped for a good looking Vauxhall Frontera four track, it was second hand but the price was way over of her present budget at Twelve thousand pounds, but she fell in love with it on first sight.

Zac got the salesman to change the tyres and replace a damaged wing mirror, but that meant she couldn't take it straight away and wouldn't be able to surprise the kids after all. Disappointed, she got in the van with her brother again for the journey back home.

He was unusually silent for a while, thinking it was something to do with the car, she asked if there was anything bothering him.

Then he dropped the bombshell.

"I don't think you are going to like this, but what with having a little too much to drink and that, I told Donna about our adventure at the grave yard...you know the ring and that," he said.

"Oh! God what did you do that for." she said, already trying to work out how she was going to explain her ghoulish behaviour to her friend.

"How did she take it?" Lisa asked worried.

" She didn't say anything but I don't think she liked it," he said, matter of factly.

Zac dropped her off at home, reflecting on what he had said, she knew she would have to tell her friend the truth.

Late that afternoon Lisa arrived at Peter Mason's office to keep her appointment at two pm. She was surprised to see a stranger sitting in front of the young bespectacled solicitor leafing through a giant sheaf of papers, thinking there had probably been a mix up with the appointment list she turned to exit.

"Ah! Mrs Whittle thank you for coming," Mason said, indicating the man sitting opposite him, he said.

"I don't think you've met Mr Wella before, but he's the accountant who has done the audit on your late husband's company, Marks and Whittle, of course,"

The tall pale faced man got up and offered Lisa his hand, saying.

"Robert Wella, pleased to meet you Mrs Whittle, Can I say how sorry I was to hear about your husband, I had met him on a few occasions in the course of business, please accept my condolences."

Lisa nodded and sat down next to him.

"You may be wondering where Mr Marks is," Mason interjected,

" Well I shouldn't be saying this, I'm acting somewhat unethical really, I've deliberately got you here earlier in order to put you in the picture... warn you, so to speak. About three months before your husband's accident the company lost a large soft- ware order in the states, they had borrowed heavily to finance the deal, then at the last moment the American company pulled out, unhappy about some of the computer programs, leaving the company in dire striates.....seriously in debt in fact."

"So serious in fact that there isn't any working capital left whatsoever, in fact the company had to borrow money to pay their three employees." the accountant added.

"Were you aware of this Mrs Whittle?" Mason asked.

"No, my husband never talked about his work much, he didn't seem worried, we had some domestic problems, but he didn't seem unduly worried about anything at work," Lisa replied.

"Well to be frank with you the reason I wanted you here at two o'clock was simply to give you some time to digest the facts, before Mr Marks is due here at half past, cutting a long story short, any settlement you quite rightly thought you would be entitled to… is simply non existent.

Lisa felt cheated, the money was of no importance to her now, but to think Martyn had invested such a huge chunk of his life, seven years of hard work down the drain. She had plenty of sleepless nights worrying with him too. He'd be crushed if he could witness this now, she thought. The finger of blame was pointing squarely at Marks, he was responsible for the programming, after all.

As if on cue, Marks rapped the door and entered. If the man had any doubt about his future prospects he didn't show it, his bearing was ramrod straight with a smug grin etched across his moustachioed face.

"Lisa! Good to see you, when did you get back from your sisters?" he asked.

Lisa didn't answer, instead she looked straight toward Mason hoping he would begin to tell him the news- take the wind out of his sails.

Introducing the accountant, he told him he was from a company, called Charterhouse, responsible for the independent audit, an old well respected family firm from Penington.

He invited him to sit down.

"I'm afraid the news is bleak for the company, I have Mr Wella's report in front of me and it doesn't make good reading, unless you can raise a capital sum, of at least, one hundred thousand pounds, by the end of the month, it will be Mr Wella's sad duty to inform the receiver."

The smug look vanished from his face, with head bowed he was unusually silent.

Then suddenly, without warning the man seemed to go ballistic, looking wild- eyed over to Lisa, he screamed,

"You...you bitch, you could save this company, you'll have the money from Martyn's life insurance, the poor devil would roll over in his grave if he could see how you're acting now. You didn't deserve him... you...you, armour suited, unemotional iron-clad excuse for a woman,"

Lisa literally leapt over, the by now cringing accountant, sitting between them, and grabbing Marks around the neck she pulled him backwards until the chair he was sitting on tumbled, crashing him down to the floor, leaving him flat on his back, shocked and frightened, staring at the ceiling.

Pinning him down, she straddled his shoulders with her knees, and pummelled his face with closed fists, drawing blood with each and every blow, shouting,

"You creep it's because of you my husband is dead, you corrupt every thing you touch you ruined your own marriage, as well as mine,"

Peter Mason had frozen rigid in his chair, but the sight of blood seemed to bring him back to his senses, screaming at Wella he said.

"For God's sake do something man."

Wella had moved into the corner, his whole body shaking, he had never witnessed anything remotely like this before, the woman's venom had shocked him into a kind of passive inaction.

The receptionist rushed in after hearing the commotion and took note of the scene, then just stood there screaming and doing nothing

By the time Mason had managed to restrain Lisa, by gabbing her arm and forcing it up her back, Marks was near to unconsciousness.

Nobody in that room would have thought it possible for a woman of five foot eight to overwhelm a heavily built man of six foot two.

Lisa was still raging, while Mason forcibly ejected her from the room still screaming, and shouting,

"I haven't finished with you yet you creep, do you hear me? I haven't finished ..."

CHAPTER 6

The next day Lisa lay in bed, nursing a swollen hand.

It's funny really, she thought, how a night's sleep, albeit a restless one, could make such a difference, yesterday she was on a high with adrenaline rushing through her veins, now this morning, she was beginning to have deep feelings of remorse.

How could she have acted like that, she questioned, it was no way for a woman to act, let alone a recently widowed one, they must think I'm some sort of crazy woman.

He's bound to press charges. Mason would insist... he'd have to, being a bastion of the law. They've probably photographed Mark's injuries already.

She could apologise of course, yet even in this conciliatory mood she couldn't imagine herself doing such a thing. If only Mason knew the true story.

If she received a summons she would have to go along with it... that's all.

No, she'd have to tough it out, keep a low profile... fat chance of that though, when people find out about her lottery win, she would try her damnedest to keep it a secret. And what about Donna, what would she say to her?

Winning the lottery at this time wasn't turning out to be easy, it was compounding events, hardly making her life easier.

At that moment Kirsty knocked on her door, shouting,

"Mummy we are going to be late for school, it's a quarter past eight."

"You can stay home today darling, I want you to come with Mummy to pick her new car." Lisa said.

"Oh! that's brill Mum, I'll go and get Ben his breakfast." she shouted excitedly, skipping downstairs.

Lisa thought it better to put yesterday behind her, the guilt she felt was more for her own behaviour than for Marks, it was obvious that nothing had been resolved with him.

Pulling herself together she went down stairs, had breakfast and got the children ready for their trip out.

They caught the early bus to Penington, planning to call in at the shop to see Donna. This business of Zac telling her friend about that ghoulish episode at the cemetery, worried her more than that crazy fracas at Mason's office

Donna was serving a customer when she tapped at the window, she beckoned them inside, and it was plainly noticeable that she didn't have her usual cheery smile.

"Hello! there got the children with you today then." she said, curtly.

"Yes I'm taking them with me to pick up my new car, they're really excited about it, anyway I couldn't take them to school- I didn't have Zac's van," she explained.

"Oh! I'm sure it must have slipped his mind he'd have brought it over if he had realised." her friend said, still sounding a little surly.

"It doesn't matter." Lisa said, picking Ben up, who, by this time, was getting a little tetchy.

"What's wrong with your hand?" Donna asked observing the band-aid as she held Ben.

"Oh! that." she said, glancing down at it, "It's nothing serious, I banged it on the table at the solicitors yesterday." Lisa added, her eyes starting to mist over.

Realising there was something seriously wrong, Donna led the kids to the little tea-room at the back of the shop, instructing Kirsty to look after Ben for a while she had a chat with her Mummy.

When she returned, Lisa was sobbing quietly.

"There's something wrong isn't there...What's the matter?" she asked, pulling over a chair, and guiding her friend to sit upon it.

"It's not because Zac told me something he shouldn't have is it?" she queried again.

"Partly that," Lisa sobbed, "I haven't been completely open with you, and you deserve that after everything you've done, it's what happened at the solicitors too!" she said sobbing now, having trouble getting her breath.

"What the heck happened there to upset you as much." Donna quizzed, trying to make sense of it.

"You're not going to believe this, but there was a fight, not just a verbal one... a real one, Boots, fists and everything, I attacked Phillip Marks, assaulted him...he wanted me to hand over Martyn's life policy money, his face ended up a real mess...full of blood, he's bound to press charges..." Lisa said, tearfully.

"Knowing that devil, he probably asked for everything he got," her friend exclaimed.

"Oh I'm not worried about him, it's just... well, I'm beginning to wonder if I'm going crazy or something, and to top it all…um' I've gone and won the blasted lottery!" she cried, burying her face in a large handkerchief.

Her friend took a tentative step backwards, perhaps she is going do ladle, imagining things. she thought.

"What do you mean won the lottery?" she asked, puzzled.

"The ticket... the winning ticket, I got it from the grave, it was buried with Martyn in his blazer pocket," she cried, sobbing freely now.

"But Zac said you done it for a ring...that bitch's ring, he'd been wearing." her friend said.

"No!…no I couldn't tell him what I was doing it for. He's a unknown quantity, even to me, and he might have grabbed it himself." Lisa cried.

Donna froze on the spot, everything was becoming clearer now. When Zac had first told her about it, she thought her friend had flipped her lid, enlisting his help to break the law and dig up a grave just for a wedding band.

She stared intently at her friend, then laughed, more out of sympathy than humour, she realised her friend had been buried under a landslide of emotional horror of late, what with her bereavement, and subsequent events, but it was plainly obvious she still hadn't realised how lucky she'd been.

"What's so funny?" Lisa asked, mopping her eyes.

"You ...you silly sausage, you are kind of crazy, aren't you?" she said, putting her arms around her, making her cry even more, as Kirsty appeared through the back door,

"Mummy Ben's being wicked, he's let the tap run and he won't let me turn it off."

Donna disentangled herself from her friend, and went back to sort out the wayward boy, Lisa, meanwhile rummaged around in her cosmetic bag searching for some powder to repair her makeup.

Calling out to Donna, she shouted,

"Look! I'm off now, we will talk later, I have to take the children for some lunch and then we are going to pick up the car."

Leading Ben by the hand, she made for the door, saying.

"By the way Don, don't mention any of this to Zac, he's a bit of a loose cannon, d'you understand... we'll keep this to our selves for the time being, I'll see you later."

As soon as they stepped on to the pavement Kirsty insisted on having her lunch at Mac Donald's.

True to form Ben started playing up as soon as they sat down in the restaurant, kicking both of them underneath the table, then just as suddenly, jumping off his chair, wandering over to a man waiting at the counter.

"Daddy!...Daddy!" he pleaded pitifully, with arms outstretched, begging to be picked up.

Lisa dashed over to collect him, but Ben remained rooted to the spot screaming that he wanted his father.

Lisa apologised to the man, who was obviously embarrassed, trying making light of it, explaining that he'd been going through a growing phase, and perceiving every tall man with fair hair, as his Daddy.

Everybody remained mute, there was no reaction at all, making her think her remark had been too flippant. How could she tell them the lad had just lost his daddy. Scooping Ben up into her arms she consoled him until he eventually calmed down, finally drifting off into an exhausted sleep.

It was proof positive that the little one was really beginning to miss his father.

Sitting near the window, she could clearly see, the building that housed Mason's office. She shuddered as she thought about the events of yesterday afternoon, wondering what kind of scene there had been after she'd been forcibly ejected.

Had they taken him to see a doctor? Did he go running to the police?

What with the firm being on the brink of bankruptcy, Marks would become even more of a wild card, even more of a danger to her, with nothing to occupy his seemingly strange obsessive mind.

It would be lovely to think that he had learned his lesson, but her intuition said the opposite. If he took the legal path, like taking out a writ, at least that would be positive behaviour… fetching everything out into the open. But knowing him, he'd seek his own cunning kind of revenge.

Not having a clue as to what the future held in store, made Lisa feel even more insecure than she already felt.

Later, relieved to step out into the fresh air, they caught a bus that took them to within fifty metres of the garage, and walked the rest of the way to the huge, sprawling motor mart, situated in the middle of a busy, out of town, shopping complex.

The salesman must have caught sight of them as soon they had entered. Trotting over to them he explained that the vehicle was ready, and requested her to follow him to his porta-cabin office.

"How much did you say you were putting down?" he enquired.

"Six thou." Lisa said," quickly, "I told you before, I'll pay the sum in two payments, you'll get the rest early next week. You haven't changed your mind have you… about the agreement I mean?

"No it's still a cash sale, like we agreed," the salesman confirmed.

Lisa scribbled out the cheque, and followed him to the compound, the keys jangling in her hand.

The Frontera looked gorgeous, a lovely metallic green colour, which had been highly polished leaving a mirror finish, she could even smell the new-ness of the tyres.

It was a rare pleasure to handle the steering wheel, its slick power steering, making easy work of the bends, and inclines on their return journey back home.

As soon as they arrived back home, Kirsty insisted that she should clean it.

Lisa despaired for the brand new coat of polish, but knew if she played along with her she'd have time to phone the Camelot office.

Taking them out to the drive, she made doubly sure they were occupied before going back inside the house to phone.

The receptionist at Tolpit's Lane, put her through to Ken Denton.

He informed her that everything had been arranged, and they were in the process of arranging a car to pick her up at ten am the following morning, in order to ferry her down to their main office at Watford.

Lisa didn't know what made her suggest it, but found herself asking,

"Can I bring a friend?"

"Of course you can Mrs Whittle, that's entirely up to you, Oh! And incidentally we are mindful of your request for having no publicity, so we'll be sending a unmarked car… so as not to attract any attention, will that all right with you? he quizzed.

"Yes, of course, that will be lovely…I will expect you around ten then," she replied, before bidding him goodbye.

She supposed she had subconsciously thought of her friend, as she still felt nervous about of all the unfamiliar events beginning to envelope her. Having Donna Marie at her side, would give her that added confidence she needed.

She rang her friend that evening, broaching the subject, and asking if she would accompany her down to Watford to collect her prize.

"Oh yes please darling…I'd love to." she said excitedly, "But what about the shop?"

"Do you think Zac could handle it for a couple of days, I think he'd be OK if he melted into the background a little. Most women will serve themselves anyway." Lisa said.

"I'll ask him later, don't worry he'll do it as long as you pay him… so we'll be away for two days then?" she questioned.

"Yes they're taking us out for dinner, somewhere private-they've booked us a room at some swanky hotel down there, the only problem is, I still haven't found anyone to mind the kids yet. Look's like I'll have to coax Pam next door again," Lisa explained.

'What are you going to wear?" Donna quizzed.

"Probably my little black dress for the dinner, but nothing to ostentatious, I don't want any photographs taken anyway," Lisa replied.

"I'll see you at ten tomorrow then." Donna concluded, ringing off.

The journey down to Watford took forty five minutes, the chauffeur, who insisted he be called cockney Bill, made it a pleasant one, he was a real east end raconteur, relating some of the episodes he had experienced with other jackpot winners, who, like her, had requested no publicity.

One man, a Scotsman, was disguised as a postman wearing sunglasses complete with mailbag, 'To shove the luvly loot in'... was the way he described it. he said.

Another, a woman... insisted on having her two million pounds prize paid in tenners. Then, as if that wasn't enough, stacked up neatly into suitcases to be carried by her two giant son's, sporting broken noses, and huge cauliflower ears that any self respecting policeman would question on sight.

As soon as they had arrived at Tolpit Lane, Mrs Haynes, and J. D greeted them. The very same people Lisa had met at the Red Lion.

"Is this your friend?" D.J. asked.

Lisa introduced her and Donna shook their hands then Mrs Haynes led the way, informing them that Denton was waiting to receive them at his office.

Kenneth Denton came across as a totally different man than the person she had met in Red Lion, cracking jokes, one on top of the other, and in no time at all he had them doubled up with laughter. Even the normally cool Mrs Haynes came over differently, pouring one glass after another of pink champagne, and drinking most of them herself.

"I didn't think you drank alcohol, you only had a tonic water at the Red Lion," Lisa observed.

"Ah! that's policy dear, we used to have a few when the lottery first started, but would you believe, some people reported us, so we find out who we are dealing with now."

After the unexpected celebration, Lisa spent over an hour with her in her office. Pouring over all kinds of financial plans, joking and giggling, with the redoubtable Mrs Haynes suggesting that if a Brewery rep came into the office right now, the smell alone would convince him they were about to purchase every pub on his patch.

Some time later cockney Bill drove them to the Metropole hotel near by, and booked them into a suite on the top floor of the six-storey building.

It was a four- star hotel, the top suite was absolutely luxurious, tastefully decorated in shades of pink and green, starting with a spacious reception area, that led into a huge oblong shaped lounge, tastefully decorated with dark oak period furniture. Off which lay two large bedrooms, situated east and west of the room, each graced with lace draped four poster canopy beds, augmented with their own en suite bathrooms, situated behind cleverly concealed doors in the wood panelling.

They spent the rest of the day ringing room service, bathing and giving each other makeovers.

Lisa deliberately dressed down, she had on he favourite back dress with a gold pendant, and three- inch block heeled shoes. Donna, on the other hand, looked outrageous, adorned, as she was, in a low cut, yellow strapless see thro' satin suit.

The dinner was a quiet, informal affair, the three course meal was served in a private room adjacent to the restaurant, the rep's turning out to be excellent company.

They had everyone in stitches, relating some of the hilarious episodes they had experienced with the ill-prepared lottery winners, from all different parts of the country, the evening finally ending up with the presentation of Lisa's cheque.

Donna though, had other things on her mind, she had been making a play for the good looking young waiter who had been attending them through the evening, and in no time at all they were entangled in a passionate embrace down at the opposite end of the room.

Lisa thought it ironical that she had won a fortune, but her friend was having all the fun. Later, her friend disappeared before making another entrance bubbling with excitement, as she placed her top coat on, making her excuses. Proclaiming she was going to spend some time with her new found friend.

Lisa spent the following day travelling around with Jenny, up at the West End on a wild shopping spree, the day ending in an anti climax, culminating with a cold and shivery tour around the city on an open-air bus.

Donna still hadn't returned, so Cockney Bill drove her back home on her own, and she wondered if she would ever see her friend again, as she tried to work out some excuse for the benefit of her little brother.

She instructed Bill to be drop her off the other side of Hunters Gate, hoping Pam or the other neighbours wouldn't see her, especially after telling everybody she was going down to visit her sister in Plymouth by train.

Lisa was sick to the back teeth of telling lies, she had hoped by now everything would have been settled, and she could finally throw off the cloak of subterfuge she'd been wearing since Martyn's death.

Collecting the children, she thanked Pam again for her kindness, and took them down to the shop in Penington to see how Zac had fared.

"Am I glad to see you Sis, I thought you said you didn't have many customers," he bleated, as soon as she entered.

"I've had at least thirty punters these last two days, and I think I've gone and messed the till up," he said again.

"What d'you mean?" Lisa said, walking over and noticing the empty till tray still open.

"Well I needed some money for lunch yesterday and the damn thing wouldn't ring up, I must have pressed two buttons at once or something, so I forced it open and stuck all the money in that draw over there...there must be about seventy pounds in all," he said, pointing to the place where they kept an assortment of tights, and children's socks.

Kirsty, listening to what was being said, went over and scooped the notes out of the draw, handing them to Lisa, giving her uncle a superior look

"Where's Donna Marie then? he asked.

"Oh! she went to see Paul her brother," she lied, "he lives down in Horhill, Southampton, hasn't seen him since they were kids she said, she'll be back in couple of days though." Lisa explained, hoping he wouldn't probe any further.

Lisa re- programmed the till, and Zac agreed to stay on for the rest of the day on condition he could stay over at her place that night.

After lunch, she took the children over to the park, and sat watching them as they played on the swings.

She knew she'd have to start building bridges before very long. Becoming fully aware of having this large amount of money was beginning to make her feel a little more confident, especially after the emotional battering she had taken of late. But a lot of uncertainty still loomed on the horizon. What direction would her bogeyman take, for example! This thought niggled her a great deal.

She thought she would pay Mason a visit afterwards. Nothing ventured- nothing gained, she had the upper hand now, and she'd use that to her advantage, but she have to prepare the ground and get all the creases ironed out first.

Young Ben started his hi- jinks again when she told him they would have to leave the park; he loved every minute there. It fast degenerated into a battle of wills, getting him out of there, was tantamount to wrestling a huge pike from a pond, bribing him with ice cream and false promises, before they could make their way over to the high street.

Parking herself and the children in front of the reception desk at the solicitors office, the girl was visibly surprised that she had turned up there again, especially accompanied by her children, she asked them all to take a seat while she went to see her boss.

She came back quickly, saying that Mason was busy attending a client and suggested she make an appointment for another day, adding that there was a letter already in the post for her.

It was plainly obvious he didn't want to see her, perhaps his letter would throw more light on the subject. It was turning out to be one of those days; nothing positive achieved…nothing going right.

Her train of thought was vindicated later, while driving out of town as she caught sight of the Courier news board from the corner of her eye, which read….

'JACKPOT WINNER! BELIEVED TO BE LIVING IN PENINGTON'

The news was like distress flare bursting over a broody night sky.

She had stressed that she wanted no publicity, somebody, somewhere must have leaked something.

Brining the car to an abrupt halt, she sprinted back towards the shop and purchased a copy of the newspaper.

Scouring through the pages, she expected to find her name somewhere, but there was nothing to be seen.

Small mercy, she thought, it seemed as if they had discovered the town where the winner lived, but not the actual winner.

She determined to get in touch with Denton as soon as she arrived home.

Gathering the mail at the front door, she noticed the by now, familiar envelope from the solicitors, but decided not to open it right away, her most immediate need right now was to get something done about the leak.

Her heart pounded, fuelled with a mixture of anger and anxiety, as she dialled the number asking for Richard Denton, the receptionist told her that he and everyone else at the office were away for the day on business, she asked if she could take a message.

"Yes tell either one of them to phone me first thing tomorrow please, tell them that the Penington Courier has found out that the jackpot winner is from the town."

"I'll have him phone you first thing tomorrow." she replied, before ringing off.

Opening the solicitor's letter, Mason informed her that Phillip Marks had decided not to take any action in regard to the assault at the office.

She felt relieved, at least there was some good news... it looked good on the surface. But she knew Mark's hadn't forgiven, nor forgot.

Zac arrived at her door at six thirty, looking whacked out.

"You did say I could stay tonight didn't you, I've got the key for Donna's, but the house is an empty shell without her." he pleaded.

"You poor boy you, anyone would think you were about to celebrate your silver wedding instead of knowing the girl for less than a week, come on in, the spare bed is still made up." Lisa replied.

Donna, phoned later that evening, luckily Zac was playing with the kids down at the opposite end of the room.

"You're not going to believe this." Lisa said, keeping her voice low.

"The Penington Courier has found out about the lottery win and they state that the winner lives in this town somewhere. But the good news is- they don't know who it is! To top it all I couldn't get in touch with Denton, he's away on business."

"Oh that sounds ominous." Donna said. "Hang on, I'll have a word with Steve, perhaps he could tell you something, he knows someone who won a prize once" she said, leaving the phone crackling.

"Hello, Mrs Whittle, I'm Steve Johnson... Donna's friend, we met the other night at the Metropole, look! I don't know much really, but a friend of a friend had the same trouble, he didn't want any publicity but the press managed to get some information about him, using devious methods, your best bet would be to keep out of sight for a while. The lottery people have a back up plan for this type of thing too, you know… putting people on the wrong track. Misinformation I think they call it, they used it with the guy my friend knows. The good news is, it all eventually died a death." he said.

Before Lisa could make any comment, Donna came back on the phone, saying,

"What do you think of him then?"

"How the heck do I know what he's like, he has a nice sounding voice, but… I've got more important things to think about right now…when are you planning to come home?" Lisa asked.

"Never! if things carry on the way they are doing, I'm in seventh heaven, keep in touch though, and let me know if you want any help," she said, dictating her new found phone number, before sounding off.

"Who was that, anyone I know?" Zac shouted, his head being held in a vice like grip by Kirsty, with Ben riding on his back.

"No, not really just a friend, from down the road." Lisa lied, adding.

"Look Zac, d'you think you could look after the shop for the rest of the week, I've got a lot of running around to do now Donna's away, you'd be doing me a great favour." .

"What's in it for me?" he queried.

"How does forty quid a day sound," she asked.

"That's OK, but with one condition," Zac said.

"What's that?" she asked.

"I can close the shop for half an hour or so in the day, to place a couple of bets on you know what," he said.

"I suppose so, beggars can't be choosers." she said, surrendering.

Lisa had thought she should visit Carrol, Phillip Marks ex wife. They had been good friends until her divorce eighteen months ago, but she had moved from the family home to Raydon, on the outskirts of Penington, taking the children, Jack and Lowery, with her.

It would be interesting to find out how her friend was doing these days, perhaps she could find out what her ex was up to, her motives weren't entirely mercenary, after all they had led the same sort of life, attending the firm's functions, Christmas party's etc., it would be interesting to find out how life has been treating her.

Carrol lived at thirty three, Rossington Road, Raydon, a suburb, near the edge of town, a district that had obviously seen better days.

It was a far cry from the luxurious detached house she had left at the exclusive Drayton Manor estate, by right she should have inherited that house, as he was the one at fault, but she had settled for the quick fix, cash and maintenance payments instead. She had paid a high price for her freedom.

Opening up the door, her friend beamed out her usual friendly, broad smile.

"Lisa! it's lovely to see you, I don't see many old friends these days, come on in."

She led the way to the living room at the far end of a long shadowy passageway, in the old Victorian house.

"I was so sorry to hear about Martyn, I thought there must have been some mistake, I just couldn't believe it at first," she said.

Lisa nodded. then Carrol went on,

"I wanted to come to the funeral but Jack had tonsillitis and I couldn't get a minder for him, I phoned you a few times but you were never there,"

"Did you? I've been very busy since the funeral, I saw your ex a couple of weeks ago and he told me you wanted to see me," Lisa said.

"Oh him! He comes around on Fridays he's allowed to have the children once a week, he told me what had happened to Martyn at the time, I've seen him once since. The creep seems very worried nowadays, said something about the company being in financial trouble, wanted me to put my house up for sale...can you believe it! I reminded him we were divorced and told him what he could do with his proposal," Carrol reported.

"That's not the half of it, because of the business connection, I've had all sorts trouble with him," Lisa said, adding quickly,

"Even had a fight- a real one, at the solicitors office...he wanted me to become his new partner and loan him money,"

"Well I'm not going to apologise for him love, I swear the man is crazy, seven good years I wasted on him, then I found out he'd been carrying on with scores of other women, I filed for divorce when I found out about the last one... tell me? has he made any advances to you... in a personal way," Carrol probed.

"Sort of...I always feel threatened by him, if he thinks for one moment that I'd be his partner, in any shape or form, he's barking up the wrong tree," Lisa explained.

"Well that's the bad news but I have some good too." Carrol said, with a smile.

"What's that then?" Lisa asked.

"I should be taking a new name before too long,"

"Oh, what's all this then?" Lisa enquired.

"Hobbs, Gerry... he's the new man in my life, I've known him for over a year now, the kids worship the very ground he walks on."

"Wedding bells?" Lisa asked.

"It looks like, and not too far in the future I hope, he's only a salesman, but he's certainly sold himself to me and the kids, you'll have an invitation as soon as we fix the date," she said.

"That's terrific, but whatever you do don't invite your ex… I'm really happy for you, if anyone deserves it, you do," Lisa said, hugging her tightly.

"Would you like some tea...coffee? Carrol asked.

"No I can't right now, I still have some errands to do, got to pick up the children, Oh, how are yours by the way?" Lisa enquired.

"Fine Jack is in the reception class at the infants, and Lowery in her last year at Wilton Primary, but they are growing up too fast." she said, before leading her friend to the door and bidding her goodbye, waving to her down at the bottom of the street.

There were two messages on the answering phone when she arrived home, Donna again, enquiring about the current events, and Ken Denton apologising for the leak. He went on to suggest she should keep well out of sight, and take a holiday.

CHAPTER 7

Purchasing their tickets in the main hall of the building. Lisa draped her sleepy son over her shoulder, and with her free hand helped Kirsty wheel the suitcase, as they travelled along the long grey corridor with painted abstracts on each wall. Then along with three other people, they squeezed themselves into a crowded lift and rode up to the departure lounge.

People were milling around everywhere, Lisa searched the nearest monitor for information. There was nothing, and walked past two more, the last one stating Paris, It was flashing a signal at the place the departure time should be, not understanding why, she asked the girl at the information desk for an explanation.

The girl picked up a internal phone, and after a short conversation explained, saying,

"The flight has been delayed an hour, the revised departure time is now thirteen hundred hours, we won't know for certain until it's up on the screen, it could be sooner than that, but we won't know until the problem has been re assessed again."

Lisa was beginning to regret coming to Heathrow; perhaps Eurostar would have been a better bet.

Relieved to unload her son off her shoulder, she sat the children down, and gave them a snack, and rummaged in her bag for a magazine, settling in for a long delay.

Fifteen minutes later she was surprised, and pleased to hear a voice announce that the passengers scheduled for the Paris flight should report to gate four.

They arrived at Charles de Gaulle airport just over one hour later, with Ben grizzling and complaining he was hungry and Kirsty complaining that all she saw were clouds.

The officer at customs never gave them a glance as they passed through the arrival building. Lisa felt relieved; she couldn't handle being stopped now, what with Ben out cold, pressing down on her like a ton weight.

A tall blonde smartly dressed man, who had spoken briefly, and helped lift her hand luggage into the storage cupboard on the plane, approached from behind and asked if he could help again, with the suitcase.

"Would you, that's very kind of you." she replied.

Taking the wheely case off Kirsty, he introduced himself.

"I'm Hamish McDonald, I hope you don't mind me asking, but are you on the way to Disney? Only I noticed that sticker on your suitcase."

"Oh! That! well that's a couple of years old now, but yes, we are going there for a week's holiday. Actually, I haven't got round to booking in yet, the kids needed a break, they've both had a trying time lately."

"You shouldn't have any trouble getting in, they take people who turn up, I'm working there this week, been commissioned to program some software for them, so I'll probably bump into you from time to time." he said.

"That would be nice." Lisa replied.

Stepping out of the building on to the sidewalk, Hamish flagged down a black Citroen taxi, and addressed the driver in French, before opening the door, helping Lisa and the children into the back seats.

"Do you mind if I share the car?" he asked.

Lisa accepted, and the journey was pleasant one, Hamish seemed very interested to hear about Martyn, and his involvement in the computer software business.

They arrived at the theme park some twenty minutes later, stepping into a world of days gone by. The streets lined with quaint old fashioned shops overlooking the busy road filled with antique cars, horse drawn street cars, even steam trains.

Hamish led them over to the main theme park booking office, and helped her as she tried to sort out a suitable hotel for her and the children.

There was a vacancy at the hotel Cheyenne, in Frontierland approximately ten minutes walking distance from the office, it had a cowboy theme and would be great for the kids, but all too soon he apologised, saying he had to leave in order to report to the company offices. He hoped he'd see them during the week sometime.

Lisa was sorry to see him go, she felt comfortable with him.

Ben was transfixed, pointing to a steam train he shouted excitedly.

"Me ride...Mummy, I want to ride." at the same time grabbing hold of Kirsty's hand, and pulling her out on to the road.

The driver stopped, and they jumped on board asking the conductor to stop at Frontier land, the children could hardly contain their excitement and seemed goggle eyed with all the magic of a by gone era surrounding them

The hotel was surrounded by a typical wild- west frontier town, with wooden walkways, verandas, Indian tepees and a log fort. All conjuring up scenes from the old black and white cowboy movies.

Lisa was pleased with the room, there was bunk beds for the children, and a three quarter bed, with a beautiful duvet depicting a cheerful scenes straight out of the old west, for herself.

As soon as they had surveyed their rooms and booked in, Kirsty complained that she felt hungry.

She took them to the hotel restaurant, a Texas style chuck wagon café, which served barbecue specialities, with French fries and a side salad.

The kids couldn't stay still for long, as soon as they had eaten Kirsty insisted on going out to see the sights again and it wasn't enough to stroll up Main street, they had to travel up and down it three times. Twice on horse drawn streetcars, with yet one more excursion on a steam train.

It was getting dark when they arrived back at the hotel, everyone was shattered, Lisa felt as if she had walked a hundred miles. Curious about what was happening at home she thought to phone, but soon realised it would be way past midnight there.

The desk clerk told her a Mr McDonald had been around, asking for her.

Sorry to have missed him, she pondered on why he wanted so soon after their initial meeting.

At breakfast the following morning, Kirsty nagged her about going to Space Mountain. Lisa finally relented, but had to phone Zac at the shop firs, or she'd never rest.

Using the public phone in the hotel lobby, she finally got through to him.

"You're early." he grunted, sounding breathless. "I heard the phone ringing just as I was opening up."

"What's the state of play back there?" she probed.

"Well I'm afraid they know who you are now. They begged me for a photograph, and information, but I've ignored them...kept out of their way" Zac replied.

"We won't be home till next Saturday, maybe the witch hunt will be off by then. Look, if they keep on asking questions, don't breath a word, understand, we can't let them find out how we got that ticket. Just imagine what they would make of that, they'd add all sorts of black magic into it, we'd never live it down," she said.

"Don't worry they'll never get it from me Sis… so you'll be home Saturday then?" Zac asked.

"Yes! oh! by the way, any news of Donna yet?" she asked.

"No, nothing, she hasn't even dropped me a line… I'll let you know when she comes back."

Arriving back at the restaurant she was surprised to see Hamish sitting there, quite happily chatting to the kids.

"Don't worry I'm not planning to kidnap them." he said, smiling and ruffling Ben's hair.

"What are you doing here this time in the morning?" Lisa asked.

"I've got the day off, I'm at a loose end really, I was hoping I could join you and the kids for the day, I tried to get in touch with you yesterday, but you were out." he said.

"What do you think kids? Would you like Mr McDonald here to come with us?" Lisa asked.

"Oh! Yes please." Kirsty said, nudging Ben, already nodding his agreement.

"There's your answer, we were planning to see Buzz Lightyear, and take a ride on Space Mountain." Lisa said.

"You'll have no trouble meeting Buzz, but the kids won't be able to take the ride." Hamish said authoritatively.

"You have to be four foot eight in height, but there's a hundreds other places, we could explore, I could take you to Fantasyland if you like."

"I think you had better address that question to the kids."she said.

Turning to Kirsty he asked, "What you say to a trip on a canal there?

Do you like the beauty and the beast, the little mermaid... we can see all that if you want."

"Oh! Yes please…can we Mummy please?" she pleaded.

"Oh! I suppose so, lead the way Macduff, you win." Lisa said, relenting.

A couple of hours into the fun trip Lisa wondered if Hamish regretted his decision, if he wasn't busily showing Kirsty the sights, then he was humping Ben on his shoulders running up and down steps and walkways, acting like an over grown kid himself.

Sometime during the busy fun day she realised she liked this tall blond Scotsman, he reminded her of Martyn, especially in their earlier years.

Twice, in the course of the day, he dropped the hint there were baby-sitting facilities at the hotel, asking if she would accompany him somewhere that night. But she refused, not feeling up to that yet.

Hamish didn't turn up the following day, but she needn't have worried, there was a message waiting for her at the desk when they returned to the hotel that evening, asking if he could repeat the experience of the day before, she couldn't help but wonder how he could take so much time off.

Some instinct deep inside told her she should call a halt to it all, she felt it was too soon for any kind of relationship, friendship or otherwise, but for the sake of the kids she knew she couldn't refuse. It was obvious they loved being in his company; he was becoming their favourite uncle, as far as they were concerned, breathing new life into them, taking their minds off their late Dad.

Early the following morning he was already waiting in the restaurant, in time to share breakfast with them.

"Where are we going today Uncle Mac?" Kirsty asked.

"How would you like to see some real nasties… horrible gungy pirates." he suggested.

"Oh! that would be great." Kirsty cried out, tugging at Lisa's arm.

They all knew then, that they were in for a fantastic day.

The wily Scot frightened them all pretending to be a swashbuckling pirate, ambushing them as they turned corners, even climbing up a rope ladder pretending to hoist the scull and cross bones.

By the time they got back to their room at the hotel Ben was out cold, sleeping in Lisa's arms, with Kirsty wanting her mother to hug her, ready to crash out too.

"How do you fancy dancing to some swinging country music tonight?" Hamish asked.

She surprised herself by saying she would.

The desk clerk arranged for a child minder to look in on them while she was out.

With the children asleep, she took a leisurely shower feeling odd about going on a date, it made her feel young again, and she felt free for the first time in a long time.

It was a respite from her mounting problems, a safe haven, an island a million miles away from her mounting, day-to-day worries.

The tall good-looking Scotsman took her to the Billy Bobs country and western club, and later ended up at the Red Garter nightclub, right next door to her hotel.

They talked and danced the evening away, she had forgotten what this world felt like, talking to Hamish was exhilarating, a nice experience. The opposite of what usually happened with Martyn, especially towards the end.

It was well after midnight when they got back to the hotel

They sat down in the lobby, Hamish took her hand and asked if she had enjoyed herself

"It was great, but it's occurred to me I hardly know anything about you yet, will I see you before we leave?"

"Well the answer to the first question is I'm a single soul these days, but that's another story, the second... I hope so, but I can't say for certain. Here! take my card... it's the address of my flat in London, and I'll write down my home address in Scotland on the back, get in touch with me there if you want." he said, scribbling something quickly on the back.

"I may surprise you yet." Lisa said, getting up to check on the children.

Hamish bent forward and kissed her gently on the cheek.

"That's for being such wonderful company." he said. Then he had gone.

She never saw him again that week, wishing she had asked him where his place of work was, because on Friday evening, after leaving the kids with a play group at the hotel, Kirsty said something that generated goose pimples, sending shivers up and down her spine.

"We played touch and hide with Lowery and Jack Mummy, and they asked where you were."

"Was uncle Phillip here too?" she asked, shocked at the disclosure.

But the both of them nodded their heads from side to side.

Sleep was out of the question, what the hell were his children doing here, surely even he wasn't that crazy, it spooked her to think that he could be stalking her.

She longed to be able to talk to Hamish, but he hadn't said where she could get hold of him. Anyway, here in the strong bright light of a new morning, she decided Kirsty had probably imagined things what with all the excitement they had experienced in recent days

Dismissing the whole episode from her mind, she signed out of the holiday centre, hopping the bus back to Paris, to the Charles de Gaul airport.

Arriving home at Penington they headed straight for Bric-a-Brac, she wanted to ask Zac if there had been any further developments with the Courier.

Lisa was surprised to see Donna there.

"You're back then." Lisa said.

"I should be saying the same to you." Donna replied, adding...

"Did you have a nice time?"

Kirsty stepped forward and handed her a model of Buzz Lightyear,

"We met Buzz," she said, excitedly.

"But he told us we couldn't ride on space mountain 'cos we were too young, we had a brilliant time with Uncle Hamish though."

"What happened with you?" Lisa quizzed.

"Oh! it was heaven for a few days, then the cheeky beggar had to spoil it all, bringing some girl home from work and even fixed some video equipment up, suggesting we make a threesome, I told him I didn't want to live in a commune and told him where he could stick his fantasies." Donna explained.

"I've got some terrific news for you too, but I'll tell you about it later, has anyone been snooping around from the local rag?" Lisa asked.

"It's too late for that... here.." she said, handing her the Thursday edition of the local paper.

Her picture was staring out at her like a large mirror reflection, on the front page, and underneath, the caption...

'PENINGTON WIDOW, SCOOPS THE JACKPOT.'

It went on to give her full name and address.

Lisa recognised the photograph, it was a holiday snap taken in Majorca three years ago.

She remembered it being taken by one of the staff at the hotel at the side of the swimming pool, Martyn and Kirsty had been on it, she wasn't much more than a baby then. They must have cut that part off, she thought.... but how did they get it?

"I'm going over to check on the house now I'll see you later." Lisa said, catching hold of the children and leaving.

Driving into the close, she saw a tall gaunt man leaning up against a small white van, he had a camera strapped around each shoulder, and yet another guy was peering into her front window. It was obvious they were reporters from some newspaper or other.

She realised then they would never give up on their quest.

Reversing the car back to the cross road at the bottom of the road, she manoeuvred it into a U Turn, and made her way back to the shop

Donna suggested she would go and face the news hounds, tell them it was useless them waiting, as she was presently abroad on holiday, and not expected back for another week.

Twenty minutes later her friend came back saying she had some good, and some awful news… the good concerned the reporters.

She said after she had confronted them saying she was a concerned friend of the owner of the house, she waited for a while, parked up near the entrance of the close and watched them depart, apparently satisfied with her explanation.

"What's the bad then?" her friend probed

"I went right up to the house." Donna said.

"Yes… so? Lisa quizzed.

"I'm afraid its been broken in to, the window at the back is smashed, and there's stuff strewn all over the kitchenette and lounge, it must have been late yesterday or early this morning 'cos I checked lunch time yesterday, like I've done every morning since you've been away." Donna explained.

"God! I don't believe this, the devil must be putting his middle finger up to me or worst." Lisa said, her eyes filling up with tears.

"I'm off I'll see you later." Lisa said, picking Ben up and moving to the door.

"Shall I come with you?" Donna asked.

"No, I'll see what the damage is, but don't call the police unless I tell you." she said, slamming the door behind her.

Filled by now with trepidation, she unlocked the front door.

There was a pyramid of mail on the floor, and most of it, looked like junk.

The lounge looked as if a bomb had hit it, all the drawers in the room had been rifled, the contents scattered every which way. Even the television had been moved, ending up over on the opposite side of the room.

She knew she couldn't face the hassle of tidying the mess up right away, so she switched on the central heating and put the kettle on. Collecting the mail, she placed it on the kitchen table and began sorting it out.

The first ten or so were begging letters, discarding these, she opened a small brown envelope, with no stamp, and felt a cold shiver course up her spine. Realising quickly that the text was spelt out in all different sized print fonts, which had obviously been cut from newspapers, it read…

SWEETHEART, YOU' RE WORTH EVERY PENNY. BUT DON'T WORRY, I'M KEEPING A BEADY EYE ON YOU.

It must be him, she thought, it has to be Marks, the kids were right, he must have been there at Disney stalking them. How crazy can someone get!

She thought of Hamish, and wondered if he was home yet, he said he'd be finished up by the end of the week, she really needed someone she could confide in.

Calling next door, she asked Pam if she could look after the kids for a couple of hours.

Her neighbour looked surprised to see her, and she asked, "Is it true what the newspaper said?"

"Yes! I was going to tell you but I had hoped to keep it secret for a while, I didn't want the children disturbed again, so soon after Martyn's accident."

"Don't worry I'd do exactly the same, look, you bring the kids around and we'll have a chat later on." Pam said.

A glum looking Zac opened up the door to her, at Cashmere Avenue.

"You're a dark horse you never said anything about a lottery ticket." he said.

"Don't start now little brother, or I'll drown in my own troubles I'll explain everything later, I wasn't sure about it myself, until I got it, don't worry it could well turn out to be the best day's work you ever did, now where's Donna?"

He took her into the lounge, her friend lay on the sofa with her feet curled up beneath her, watching the TV.

"Hi! Is it bad? she asked.

"To be honest I haven't checked everything out properly yet, but something else has happened, something even more sinister, do you want to hear it. Like your news, there's good and bad too. " Lisa explained.

"Ok! tell me the good first then." her friend quipped.

"Well just before I got back to trouble town here, I met someone nice, a tall, good looking Scotsman. I didn't encourage him in anyway and it's a bit too soon, but he's really got my heart beating faster, and the kids absolutely adore him," she said.

"So that's what your daughter meant when she mentioned Uncle Hamish! What do you mean it's a little soon, as long as it's right for you, who the hell cares." her friend said.

Zac made an entrance from the kitchen offering them a mug of tea, and a plate of assorted biscuits.

"You've got him well trained." Lisa said, winking.

"And the bad?" Donna asked.

"Marks has been stalking me again."

Her friend looked taken aback.

"He turned up at Disney, well according to kids anyway, they nor I, didn't see him personally, but they were adamant that they were playing with Jack and Lowery at the play centre there, I didn't believe them at first, but I've just picked this letter up at home stating that he's been watching me…stalking me. Here… take a look." she said, handing it to her.

"Are you sure this is from him?" Donna asked.

"Who else could it be?" she replied.

"Do you want Zac to go round and warn him off?" she suggested.

"No, that kind of thing makes him worst, I think the best thing I could do would be to disappear for a time again, I really hate to ask, but do you think you could take care of the children for me just one more time." she asked.

"Don't tell me…you've just got to see that luscious Scotsman of yours." Donna said.

"Well it's a way of killing three birds with one stone…getting away from my stalker, escaping the press, and that break in, you name it, she said.

Zac who had been listening on the other side of the room butted in.

"I don't mind Sis, as long as you leave us that handy four track of yours."

"OK!" Lisa said. "But I'd like you both to stay at my place, at least the kids will feel at home in their own surroundings, is that OK with you?"

Zac and her friend agreed, suggesting she leave secretly, just in case Marks was keeping tabs on her.

Later, after collecting the children from Pam's, she rang Hamish's home number.

A woman answered, and asked her to wait a while, saying he had just come in, and she'd get him.

Seconds later Hamish spoke.

"That was quick. I only got back from Paris a couple of hours ago."

"I was wondering if I could come up to see you, for the weekend perhaps." she asked.

"Certainly, my, er…sister's here at the moment but she'll be gone by the morning…. how will you get here?"

"I thought by train, it's too far to drive, I thought I could leave tomorrow," she said.

"OK! If you ring me when you leave, I'll meet you at the railway station in Glasgow.

How are the kids, by the way?" he added.

"Oh they're OK they're with a friend, I'll look forward to seeing you then." she said before hanging up.

Lisa slept most of the way up to the Queen Street station in Glasgow, and apart from two changes of train, and a talkative Presbyterian minister, lecturing her about the collapse of modern day morals, the journey had been uneventfully boring.

She had rang Hamish before setting off but the woman answered again, saying she would pass on the message, Lisa hoped she would leave before she got there.

Hamish was waiting in the entrance hall of the station when she arrived, she was glad when he relieved her of her heavy hold all, placing it in the boot of his blue Vectra.

"I didn't think I'd see you so soon." he said, moving off, finding a gap in the traffic.

"It's not too soon is it?" she pressed.

"No I don't mean that, Magg's didn't get the message to me until late, so I rang the station and they had me believing you'd be up on a later train, then I found out different and rushed over here." he explained.

As he finished speaking a white Transit van cut right in front of them, forcing Hamish to put his foot on the brake.

"You stupid Sassenach idiot!" he shouted, thumping the steering wheel, in an almighty rage.

Lisa hadn't seen this side of him before, it scared her, but she reasoned the traffic could make a Saint swear.

The traffic thinned out a little as the drove past scores of grey looking high- rise apartment blocks.

"How long d'you plan to stay?" Hamish asked.

"How long would you want me to." Lisa said smiling.

They travelled on another quarter of an hour or so, then turned left and entered a long street of terraced houses, finally stopping at the top of the road.

"This is it, Gerradie Street, number Sixty Six." he said, jumping out to retrieve her hold-all from the boot.

She was surprised that he lived in a terraced house, for some odd reason she had envisaged him living in a detached suburban setting.

"Do you live here alone?" she asked.

"Of course I do, what makes you think otherwise? Oh! you mean Maggi I expect,

She stays here when I'm away on business sometimes that's all," he said.

Lisa thought his reply a little odd as she could see various items of feminine clothing lying around. But dismissed it, remembering what he'd said about his sister holding the fort while he was away.

Taking her coat and folding it over his arm, he said,

"I expect you could do with a drink, Is it the same poison?" opening up a drink's cabinet door, which switched an interior light, lighting up an array of different coloured bottles.

"Yes, with some lime and lemonade would be nice." she said, noticing a half bottle of Smirnoff on the bottom shelf.

"You're not in kind of trouble are you?" he asked, as he passed over a tumbler.

"What on earth makes you think that?" she asked.

"It's just that you seem more serious than you were, like as if you have something on your mind." he explained.

"I was on holiday then, anyway, I could say that about your fit of road rage this afternoon." she retorted.

"Oh! that, I don't seem to have had five minutes to myself lately, been rushing everywhere. I'm a bit on edge that's all," he said.

"Anyhow, you must have a lot of questions you'd like to ask, I must appear as some kind of mystery man to you." he elaborated.

"You told me you were free now, does that mean you were married at one time?" she asked.

"Twice, actually. I lived in London once, Hammersmith, had a flat in Du Cane road behind the Scrub's, that was my first attempt in the matrimonial stakes, then I found out she'd been two timing me with a screw from the big house itself." he explained.

"Were you young then?" Lisa asked, intrigued.

"Twenty four, too young some would say, made the same mistake again a year later though, not too far from here in fact, in Paisley. Two kids that time, so you can see I'm not what the world would term as a successful house husband."

"What about you?" Hamish asked.

"One marriage, one love... but he was taken from me nearly three months ago now, in a freak car accident." Lisa said, her voice faltering, tears clouding up her eyes.

Hamish stood up and walked behind her, and placed his arm around her shoulder.

"Enough of this inquisition, what do you say to a bite to eat, I know a natty little pub come restaurant in the country, at Old Monklands. What do you say we go up there?"

She nodded, at the same time fishing out a hanky from her bag mopping her moist eyes.

Hamish filled in many more gaps in his eventful life over their meal at the restaurant. Nothing he said made her doubt him she was attracted to him for some reason. he was older, five years by her reckoning, but she felt right in his company.

A middle-aged couple in the candlelit booth next to them got up and left, making them the last people in the restaurant.

"Would like to dance?" Hamish asked, getting up and offering her his hand.

"It's getting late, d'you think we should?" Lisa said, looking and wondering if anyone was watching.

"I'll be the judge of that." he said, pulling her up into his arms and shuffling to the background music.

He held her tightly against his swaying body, her heart pounding until her breathing became heavier, staring into her eyes he stopped suddenly, and pressed his lips against hers, releasing her pent up emotions that longed to be satisfied.

"Don't, please, not now." she said, pushing him away.

Hamish stood back and apologised, taking her back to the table.

"I'm sorry I thought you were of the same mind." he said.

"It's me, my fault, don't blame yourself, it's just too soon." she said.

He collected their coats and drove back to Gerradie Street.

Hamish had placed the key into the lock, and the door opened, revealing a small, surly sounding woman.

"You're late." she said. Lisa recognised the voice as the woman who had answered her on the phone.

"Maggi! what are you doing here?" he asked.

"Broggi, he's upset and wants to see you immediately," she explained.

"Not again." Hamish blurted. "Don't he ever let up, I'll have to go I suppose."

"And you are Lisa I presume." Maggi said.

Lisa nodded.

"Show her to the spare room will you Mag's." then turning to Lisa he said.

"I'll explain later."

Maggi didn't say a lot, as she led the way upstairs, it made Lisa fee even more of a stranger than she was. Slamming an open door noisily directly on top of the landing, she led the way and opened a door to a small room at the end of it.

"This is you room hen." she said, walking in and drawing the curtains across a small sash window, overlooking the street.

"The sheets are clean I changed them myself this morning," she said, already stepping back out on to the landing.

"I expect you're tired after your journey hen... so I'll bid you good night, I'll see you again sometime." she said from top of the stairs.

As soon as the woman had gone Lisa went downstairs again and made herself a cup of coffee, waiting for Hamish to return.

But he didn't come back.

She explored the rest of the house, trying to get a better picture of things, before returning to her room, but not before she opened the door that Maggi had slammed shut.

Inside the room, there was a double bed, the bedclothes thrown every which way, and two obvious indents in the pillows.

It was obvious to Lisa that two people had recently spent some in it.

She felt a torrent of anger well up inside her, he hadn't been telling her the truth.

Descending the stairwell again she made straight for the drink's cabinet and the bottle of Vodka, pouring herself a giant measure, ignoring the lime and Lemonade, she sat down, nervously glancing at the clock.

It was a quarter past three…Nothing is what it had seemed, she thought.

CHAPTER 8

The big man was visibly annoyed as Hamish entered his apartment, on the eighth floor, of the run down tenement building at Easterhouse.

His huge tattooed arms and neck, conspicuous, next to his grubby white singlet, that hardly covered his massive hairy chest.

"What the hell do you think you're playing at?" he shouted. "We agreed to stick her in dark room, instead, Mag's tells me on the phone that you take her out to dinner,"

"She's soft on me man, she came up here quicker than we thought, on her on volition, there's no need to bang her up yet. We should play this cool, I think it would be wiser." Hamish explained.

"No! you, stupid man, we haven't got the time, we're playing for big stakes, we do it properly or not at all, OK?" Broggi ordered. Pouring out two generous measures of neat whiskey.

Hamish eyed up his companion with some trepidation, he knew it wasn't wise to disagree with him, his tough reputation preceded him in every nook and cranny of the city, as well as a fair few places south of the border. But secretly, he had got to like Lisa and the kids, it was something he hadn't anticipated, not part of the equation, but his fear of Broggi was beginning to stifle any compassionate notions.

There was a short rat tat tat on the door, the big man gave him a deliberate glancing blow with his shoulder as he rushed past, opening it a couple of inches.

"It's me," a woman's voice said.

Hamish recognised the voice as Maggi's, and wondered why she had come, he had given strict orders for her to stay at the house with Lisa.

"I've come around to see what's happening, I thought the plan was that you were going to take her as soon as she arrived," she said excitedly, looking at the two men in turn.

"No the plan's the same, it's your boyfriend here, he seems to have gone a little soft in the head about the hen," Broggi said.

"I told you to stay and keep an eye on her, she'll probably scout around the house now...she'll be suspicious," Hamish warned.

"Well if she does it'll be down to you, not following orders," Maggi retorted.

"Never mind all that now, I want you to stop all this pussyfooting around, get back over there and tell her the truth…. tell her what we're about, understood!" Broggi shouted.

He knew when Broggi meant business, there was a kind of granite edge to his voice, so he didn't ague as he led the way down the graffiti covered staircase.

Maggi rode back with Hamish in his Vectra, arriving at Gerradie Street just as a red blanket of cloud caressed the horizon, relentlessly squeezing the remnants of the night sky ever upwards, Hamish wondered if it was too late, perhaps Lisa had fled by now.

He couldn't help but wonder if she was there, she would, in all probability, attack him as soon as he entered the house, but the atmosphere outside gave him no clues, it all seemed deathly quiet.

Maggi followed him through the hall and up the stairs to the box room. Opening the door quietly they were both surprised when they realised she wasn't anywhere to be seen, the bed hadn't even been used, still neatly made up.

'I've blown it,' Hamish said out aloud.

'It looks like you have you wally, I dread to think what Broggi will do now.' Maggi said, accusingly.

Hamish descended the darkened stairwell again, leaving Maggi sitting on the edge of Lisa's bed, twisting her hands together in a mood of despair.

Hamish groped along the wall, searching for the switch to turn the living room light on, then entered.

There she was… sprawled out on the settee with one arm hanging over clutching a half empty bottle of Vodka, resting on the floor, obviously in a drunken stupor.

He shouted up to Maggi of his discovery, but she spat back vindictively

'The hen knows everything, all the clippings and photo's are spread out on your bed, you great wally'

'Never mind that now, get down here quick to the living room.' he ordered.

Maggi rushed down to the living room, shouting excitedly,

'Thank god we've got her, why the hell didn't she make a run for it while she had a chance.'

'Anger I expect.' he said, bending down and struggling to lift the limp body of Lisa off the settee.

'At least we've avoided all the drama, let's get her upstairs quick.' he ordered.

Maggi the lead the way into the bedroom, Hamish followed, placing her gently on to the bed.

'Shall we move the wardrobe?' she asked.

'No, she'll be out for hours yet, just make sure she's locked up that's all.' he directed.

Returning to the living room, he poured himself a measure of his twelve year old malt, pondering on what had made her stay, obviously the hen must have known, that she'd been tricked…maybe she couldn't come to terms with how easily she had been taken in, and decided to stay, risking the danger, needing and wanting a explanation.

I would too, Hamish thought.

Maggi came down stairs to use the phone in the hall, he knew she was making a report to Broggi.

'What did he say?' he asked, as she entered.

'Nothing much, he's pleased, he'll be over in the morning, oh! And he told me to keep an eye on you.' she said.

'Do you think she'll have any looks on me after this?' Hamish asked.

'She won't… but I dare say you still have.' Maggi spit back, vindictively.

He stood up and swallowed the remainder of his drink, telling her he was going to get a duvet, and take it to Lisa in her room.

"She be cold there…" he said

Maggi jumped on him before he could complete the sentence.

'Don't expect me to join you, I warn you now Hamish McDonald, this arrangement could well turn out to be permanent.' she shouted.

Maggi had reported accurately about the clippings etc, but she hadn't described the actual state of the bedroom

Every drawer in the chest of drawers had literally been thrown to each corner of the room, the contents scattered everywhere, cluttering up every square foot of floor space.

She must have systematically rifled through everything in the room until discovering his briefcase, then forced the lock on it, with the kitchen knife, still lying on the floor.

And at the top of the bed, on the pillow was her photograph, staring out at him from an old crumpled copy of the Penington Courier, her smiling face, beginning to haunt him yet again.

Early the following morning, the rat tat tat sound of repetitive knocking, woke Hamish with a start, getting focused, he realised the din was coming from Lisa's room at the end of the landing.

Pushing his feet into worn out sandals, he used as slippers, he shuffled heavily across the landing, and parked himself outside her door.

"Keep the noise down, you'll wake up the whole neighbourhood, its not even light yet." he said.

"That's what I'm trying to do you bastard, I know your little game now, I order you to open this door now, right now!" Lisa screamed.

"Relax I'll go down and get some tea… it'll give you time to calm down, maybe then I'll open up," he said.

Hamish went downstairs, Maggi had spent the night on the sofa, she lay there, bleary eyed, propping herself up on one elbow.

"Surely now you can see what a mess you've made of all of this, you great ape, she won't take this lying down," she said.

"There's nothing for it we'll have to rush her…restrain her! she's like a crazy woman we'll just have to put her to the dark room." he instructed.

Maggi jumped up and went into the kitchen and came back up almost immediately with at roll of masking tape and several lengths of green nylon cord.

"Have you got the key?" she asked.

"Yeah! It's in the draw here." he said, rummaging around, producing a key ring with several keys in all shapes and sizes.

He knew he had to act immediately; it was obvious it wouldn't be too long before she'd vent her anger on to the window overlooking the street.

He led the way up on to the landing, and stood outside the door, winking at Maggi,

"I've brought you some tea." she said, on cue.

"Oh! you too! It doesn't take a genius to work out your little part is in this game…and as for your tea, stick the stuff where you'd normally deposit your bodily fluids you bitch," Lisa screamed.

While the women were screaming insults at each other Hamish turned the key in the lock, and giving his girlfriend another nod, and they literally crashed through the door, spinning their hapless captive off balance, toppling her on to her bed. Hamish jumped on her, pinning her down by her shoulders, then manhandling her he got her on to her stomach, lifting her arms up until the palms of her hands met.

Maggi completed the job, quickly wrapping the tape around her wrists, binding her ankles with the nylon cord.

Hamish dragged the small oak wardrobe towards the window, revealing another door, taking hold of Lisa's shoulders, he directed Maggi to lift up her feet, then the both of them dragged her into the dimly lit windowless room, dumping her unceremoniously on to a grubby rough-hewn mattress.

Lisa still kicked and struggled, the rage inside her was having a negative effect, a wasted effort that was crushing her spirit, she became aware she had to exercise some measure of control over her emotions, and fought back trying hard to stifle the fear, and panic that threatened to overwhelm her.

Her silence seemed to initiate some compassion later, on the part of Hamish, who took a penknife from his pocket and cut the tape around her wrists.

That should make things a little easier for you. But don't undo the leg ties or you'll get me into trouble," he ordered, much to the annoyance of Maggi, who, by now had a murderous look across her face.

Nothing more was said, the pair departed, slamming and bolting the door behind them before rolling the wardrobe back into place.

Slowly, but painfully she managed to sit up and surveyed her sparse surroundings.

She noticed the lamp first, emanating an eerie reddish glow.

The infra red lamp was situated above a small table, with black plastic trays spread out upon it, next to that... her bed, and in the corner, a filthy looking wash basin, which in all probability had ten years of grime upon it.

Scattered around on the floorboards below, were torn fragments of paper, discarded photographs, crumpled and spread around like discarded cinema tickets after a matinee. Leaning over, she picked up a few, and immediately recognised a part image of her daughter, it was Kirsty alright, a snap she had taken herself, three weeks after Martyn's accident, it was taken at her daughters birthday party held in Pam's next door. Memorable because it was the first time the children had smiled since before the tragedy, she picked a couple more fragments and discovered a part picture of Ben this time, a rear view, but unmistakable, she'd know him in a crowd...it was her son alright.

It got Lisa wondering if she had been their first and only victim, they had obviously done their homework concerning her family.

With hindsight, it was easy to see that it was they, who engineered the break in at her house, she began to realise how naive she had been, concerned, as she was, with her main obsession, Marks, and all the rest of it. She hadn't placed the kids squarely into the big picture; it's plain to see they are planning to use them as an emotional lever later in the game.

She glanced around her surroundings yet again, there wasn't a window, nor a slat of light even, beneath the door she had entered through, this truly was a prison in the best sense of the word.

Exhausted, she collapsed down on to the filthy mattress, searching her mind for some kind of hope…something, she could use, obviously she wouldn't cooperate, and she would make things as awkward as she could, and wait patiently until they made a mistake.

Just a chance, that's all she wanted… a chance to escape.

Her friend had been gone almost a week, and Donna was getting worried.

She had promised to keep in touch, phone the kids every day but there hadn't been a word, should she get in touch with the police, or make a few enquiries of her own.

She decided on the latter, knowing the local press were still snooping around.

As soon as she got home in the evening she blurted out her fears to Zac.

He thought that Marks had something to do with her disappearance, but Donna disagreed… only last week Carrol, Philip Mark's ex- wife, had dropped into the shop, saying that her ex had been making a nuisance of his self coming around the house, when he been ordered by the courts, to keep away.

Eventually, they both agreed he should pay Mr Marks a visit, warn him off. Try to find out if he could shed any light on their friend's disappearance.

Early the following morning Zac turned up on Mark's doorstep, in the up-market Drayton Manor estate, north of town. The tall dark moustachioed man appeared completely wrong footed as he opened the door, dressed in a smart grey double breasted suit, obviously ready to go out somewhere.

With obvious impatience, he muttered,

"What do you want, I can't loiter I have an important engagement to keep, what is it you want man?"

Zac came straight to the point.

"You don't know me, but you bloody well will do before very long, I'm Zac Tinsley, Lisa's step brother, I've got a few questions to put to you, and I want them answered truthfully, I think you know what I mean,"

Mark's looked surprised as he glanced furtively up and down the road, before indicating Zac should follow him inside the house.

He led the way into the kitchen, the light still on.

"I...I didn't realise Lisa had a brother." He blurted out.

"It seems to me that realisation of any kind, isn't part of your makeup," Zac said, his face now, six inches away from his frightened host.

"I want you to answer this, and answer truthfully, do you understand?

Were you and your children at Disneyland, Paris about a fortnight ago?" he asked.

"Two weeks you say...er'... yes, I was as a matter of fact." he stuttered.

"So it was your kids who played with Lisa's children?" Zac probed, his voice sounding more aggressive now.

"Yes they told me they did, but it's not what you think, I wasn't there stalking your sister, I took the kids for a weekend holiday there that's all," Marks replied.

"So Lisa's kids weren't lying then," Zac interrupted.

"No, but you have to believe me, it was pure chance we happened to be there at the same time as Lisa and her children." Marks said.

"What about the letter you sent her then?" Zac asked.

What letter?" Marks said, looking genuinely surprised, before turning and pouring himself a glass of water, from the mixer tap behind him.

"I don't know anything about a letter," he added, taking a gulp from the glass.

For some inexplicable reason Zac believed him this time .

"Ok! I'll give you the benefit of the doubt on that one, but I don't believe it was a just a chance meeting at Disney...I can't swallow that," he said.

"Did Lisa send you around here?" The tall man asked, obviously trying to sthe heat out of the situation.

"What the hell has that got to do with anything," Zac said, trying hard to ignore growing feelings of aggression and hatred for the man.

Marks realising Zac was about to explode, blurted out.

"OK! all right, I found out that Lisa was going on holiday from Lowery, she'd been told by a friend of a friend...'cos it was Disneyland, you know what kids are like.

It got back that's all. I arranged with Carrol to take the kids for a break at the same time, but I didn't actually talk to Lisa, every time I got near her she was with a friend, a big chap with cropped blond hair, I didn't even get to talk to the kids, but hand on heart this letter business is nothing to do with me, I don't know anything about that."

Zac continually clenched and unclenched his fist behind his back, trying to ward off his basic instincts, and heed what Donna had said, that there wasn't to be any violence.

"I should put you down right here and now you creep, but I don't think you're worth the effort, her disappearance is probably down to your unnatural behaviour anyway, but I warn you, don't ever bother my sister again. If you do you'll make sure you won't be in any fit shape to even talk to another woman, do you understand?" Zac said, pushing the ashen-faced Marks against the kitchenette work- top. Before turning, and marching quickly through the door, and on to the drive.

Zac reported back to Donna, she seemed satisfied that Marks didn't have a hand in her friend's disappearance, and relieved that someone had at last confronted him and hopefully frightened him off from stalking her friend in the future.

But it wasn't to be.

Mid morning the following day, Zac had a call from the man himself at the shop.

He tried to hang up at first, but something Marks said made him hand the receiver over to Donna.

"What!" Donna shouted, surprise etched across her face.

"Well you'd better come over then… come over to the house this evening…I'll see you then." she concluded.

"What the hell are you doing inviting that creep over," Zac asked.

"He reckons he knows who that McDonald is, says he'll tell us more this evening." she explained, as she rang up the till and counted the takings, as if trying to will the rest of the day away.

At seven sharp the doorbell rang, and Donna answered it, leading Marks into the lounge, beckoning him sit on the settee.

Zac stayed out of sight upstairs, not wanting him to feel threatened in anyway.

The tall distinguished, looking man placed a briefcase on the coffee table in front of him, tapping it with his forefinger he said, quietly,

"When I was at Disney I had the feeling I'd seen Lisa's companion before, then when Zac told me she had disappeared, something prompted me to search through some data bases I have stored, a comprehensive list of personnel in the software business, just in case I needed to poach someone in the future. I haven't got a photograph of him but I faintly remember meeting the guy at a business convention at Willesden about eight years back, he said he worked for a software company called Appro, PLC, based in Glasgow.

I had put his name and address down, on my data base, amongst others. Back then he lived at Du Cane road, Hammersmith and later that evening I called the number, as a matter of curiosity, but the current tenant there, a Mr Gerald Hammond, had no recollection of anyone with that name or description."

"Well that's something to be going on with anyway," Donna said leafing through his database lists, noticing the name Hamish McDonald's highlighted in yellow.

"It came to me later that I should have asked him if the flat was rented," Marks cut in.

"Why?" Donna asked, looking puzzled.

"Well maybe the landlord is the same one that rented it to McDonald, if so, perhaps he has a forwarding address,"

Donna looked perplexed, and enquired why he was taking all this time and trouble to pursue something that had nothing to do with him.

"Surely you should know by now that Lisa hates your guts, not to mention her brother Zac's feelings towards you. he'd willingly kill you at a drop of a hat,." she said

Marks looked down at the floor in silence for a few seconds before engaging Donna with a hypnotic stare. Saying,

"I know you'll find this hard to believe but I love Lisa, she doesn't see it the same way I know, but I'd move heaven and earth for her if she's in any danger."

"I don't know about that. Just 'cos you've presented us with some information, d'you honestly think that cancels out all the pain and misery you've put her through," Donna retorted, angrily.

"All I ask is that you keep an open mind, you know where to get in touch with me, if you need me." Marks said, standing now, reaching to the floor for his briefcase.

As soon as Donna had shown him out through the door, Zac appeared at the bottom of the stairwell.

"I heard some of what he said, but what was that he said about a database?" he asked.

Donna handed over McDonald's former address in London that she had hurriedly scribbled down.

"That's where Lisa's mystery man used to live back in the early nineties, that's all we got, but at least we're not completely out in the cold, we know Lisa was making her way up to Scotland, so we've got some kind of a start to work on at any rate,." she said.

The day following, Zac, being much more sceptical about Marks than Donna was, phoned the same number in Hammersmith that Marks had said he'd rang the previous evening, and the message on the answering machine came from someone named Hammond, which had vindicated what Marks had said.

One up for him, he thought, but he still didn't trust the man.

"What's the next move?" he shouted over to Donna, who was in the back room making tea.

"I think you will have to go down there, Philip gave me the idea, find out if the flat is owned and rented by the same person or organisation it was when McDonald was there," she replied.

"Philip now is it, it didn't take him long to cast his dark spell on you," Zac retorted.

"Don't be silly Zac, you have to agree that he knows how to go about this type of thing.

"Look! take the Frontera, get down to Hammersmith and ask some questions, see if you can find out more." Donna shouted, still out of sight.

As soon as he had departed she picked up the phone and put her thoughts into action.

"Philip I'm taking you up on your offer of help, Zac has gone down to Hammersmith to see if he can gleam a bit more information, but I don't think we are going to get too far with this line of enquiry, we obviously need someone like yourself who knows their way around... I'm thinking of Lisa of course."

"OK! leave it to me and I'll see what I can find out," Marks replied.

"Oh! And by the way, this conversation hasn't happened as far as Zac is concerned. D'you understand?" Donna concluded, replacing the receiver.

She spent the rest of the day working at the shop, returning home early evening, and had only been home ten minutes when Zac pulled up outside.

"Nothing much to go on," he shouted, throwing his coat over the stair banister.

"I had a word with that chap Hammond, and he told me that his landlord, is a letting agency called BHA, the Beta Housing Association, he'd been living there just over three years himself, and found out from the older tenants there that this was the third change of ownership since the late eighties, it's become a bit of a joke amongst the tenants there.

He said he thought the person that owned the apartments at the time McDonald lived there, had long since departed to that agency in the sky, 'cos the agency went bust leaving no written records," Zac explained.

"Is that all?" Donna probed.

"No, he told me to have a word with a Mr Kula in the basement, as he had worked for most of the landlords as a kind of caretaker come handyman, for years

I had to wait over an hour before he turned up, but he remembered him alright.

He said he'd lived there for about eighteen months, leaving around August ninety four, he remembered it clearly, because the police had arrested him and he never came back, the flat was empty for about a month after that, but he turned up again, a few years later, and offered the tenant some money to use the address as a mail drop.

Then when I asked him if he could recall if the man spoke with a Scots accent, he said he thought he had.' A funny kind of accent was the way he described it' The last time he'd seen him was about a year ago, around the apartment block there, he's assumed he was picking up his mail.

"Well at least we've established that our mystery Scotsman once lived there, it's not much to go on, but the next step is obvious." Donna suggested.

What's that?" Zac asked, looking puzzled.

"A trip up to Scotland, the problem is we don't really know if Lisa is up there, she set out for the place, but it doesn't necessarily mean that's where she landed up," Donna replied.

"Well if it north of the border… it's a lot bigger than what it appears on the map.

 I worked for a firm out of Manchester, driving an Artic delivering engineering parts, and we went to all sorts of weird out of the way places. Don't forget, there's thousands of islands strewn all around the coast there too." Zac explained.

Over the next couple of days, Zac and Donna kept up their normal routine as if on auto pilot, their minds in a totally different location than their bodies, there weren't any new leads, clues or solutions… nothing, not even any communication from Marks.

But on day three, something did occur, an incident, which, if had it gone the other way could well have developed into a Greek tragedy.

The day had started normally enough, Zac left the shop around half past three to pick up the kids from their schools, he picked Ben up first then went on to Wilton primary about a mile away in order to collect Kirsty.

He waited outside but when she didn't come out, Zac went in asked the teacher at the entrance, she confirmed Kirsy had already left with a girl called Claire Winston, she had watched them walk out through the gate.

Zac hurried back to the Frontier and patrolled up and down the road hoping he's catch up with them, assuming they had decided to walk home.

About two hundred meters further up the road he saw Kirsty and her friend being consoled by a strange man, the both of them obviously in some distress. Stopping he found out the man was Claire's Dad, who explained he was on his way to pick up his daughter from school, when a car speeding in the opposite direction caught his attention, it's horn sounding out a continuous blast, and as he glanced he caught sight of his daughter wrestling, it seemed, with the steering wheel, he gave chase, and the red car came to a halt in there, he said, pointing to the lane opposite. They were trapped it was a dead end, then as he approached the car a man and woman jumped out, and escaped over the back gardens, leaving the girls at the scene.

Kirsty was inconsolable by this time and hugged Zac until he had difficulty getting her breath. Everybody agreed that it had been a kidnap attempt.

Simon, Claire's father used his mobile to get the police on the scene and they inspected the abandoned car before taking them down to the station to make statements.

Back at home it took an eternity to calm Kirsty down, but some gentle questioning by Donna it became very revealing.

She asked her if she had ever seen the man and woman before.

"No!" she said, but they were very friendly, and the both of them talked with a nice accent,"

When Donna asked her what it sounded like, Kirsty revealed,

"The same kind of accent that Uncle Hamish had."

CHAPTER 9

Philip Marks was as unpredictable as Lisa had always said he was, as he rang and asked if he could speak to Zac.

Donna lied, saying he wasn't available, and Zac was encouraging her, miming signs from across the room. Undeterred Marks told her to tell him to meet him at, of all places a tearoom at, Sauchiehall Street, Glasgow, at the earliest opportunity, as he had a lead. He'd been up there two days, and had found out something very interesting with regard to Lisa's disappearance.

Replacing the receiver, Donna found herself mumbling,

'That man is as unpredictable as a circus clown.'

"What did he have to say?" Zac asked.

"He wants to see you," she replied.

"Is it something to do with Lisa… if it is I'll get over to his place tonight," he said.

"No! You won't, he wants you to meet him, and wait for it! at a tea room, at Sauchiehall street, in Glasgow, " she explained.

"What? What the hell is he doing up there!… when?"

"Right away I suppose, he reckons he's found out something important," Donna said.

"What about the kids?" he asked again.

"You could drop them off with Lisa's Dad, Eric, on the way up, its not too far out of the way, I'm sure Barbara would want to see them," she suggested.

"Yeah! I suppose so, d'you I think I should get going right away?" he asked.

"No tomorrow morning will be soon enough, that will give me time to talk to Kirsty, explain why she and Ben need to stay at their Grandpas for a while," Donna directed.

Seven am the following morning Zac was sitting in the Frontera ready to go, he rolled down the window and kissed Donna on the cheek.

"Now don't do a Lisa on me, phone me everyday, understand, and don't tell Eric what the real trouble is, it will only worry him, we'll tell them the truth later OK." Donna said, taking a step back on to the kerb.

The journey up to Altringham was uneventful apart from a long detour looking for a toilet stop for Ben, and a call on the mobile from Donna, telling him that Marks had called, asking if he was on his way up.

Arriving in Cherrygrove Avenue, Eric opened the door to them, and got into a flap as soon as he saw the children.

"What's wrong, where's Lisa." He asked.

"Nothing's wrong." Zac said, picking Ben up, and taking Kirsty's hand, leading them into the house.

"Lisa's gone up to Scotland, she met some chap in Paris after taking the kids for a short break at the Disney resort there, we didn't want her to go, but she was adamant, she seems really hung up on him," Zac said, remembering to follow Donna's instructions, to keep as close to the truth as possible.

She rang us a couple of days ago and asked if it was possible to extend her stay for a week or so, that would have been OK with us but Donna has been on jury service all last week and I'm finding it nigh on impossible to manage the kids and the shop, that's why I brought them up, I should have given you some notice, I hope you don't mind,"

"I don't think Barbara will, in fact I think she'd welcome the chance to have the kids for a while, she's gone shopping with Shirley, next door, can you stay a while until she comes home?" Eric asked.

"No! I can't really, I've had to lock the shop up, Donna has been picked for jury service and the case looks like going on for a couple of weeks yet," Zac lied, feeling more and more deceitful the longer the conversation went on.

"I think it will be alright really, but what about their schools, what will they say?" Eric quizzed.

"Oh! Don't worry about that, they've been terrific, really understanding since Martyn's accident, I don't think there'd be any trouble there, it will only be for a week or two anyway, " Zac said, feeling relieved now Eric had shown some interest.

Zac entered Glasgow at junction eighteen off the M77 a couple of hours later.

Ten minutes before, he'd been surprised receiving a call from Marks on his mobile, telling him he was waiting at their rendezvous. He didn't know why, but he felt angry Donna had passed his number on.

Feeling tired with the long monotonous drive up, he cruised around the city centre searching for a parking meter but couldn't find one, finally ending up at a multi-storey on George Street.

Relieved, for once, to leave the car and stretch his legs, he walked the whole length of Sauchiehall Street, and finally found the Willow Tea rooms.

The place was crowded, but he spotted Marks sitting in a corner at the far end of the room, by himself, half hidden behind a copy of The Glasgow Herald.

Pulling a chair up by the side of him, he asked.

"What's the big mystery, why have you dragged me all the way up here?"

Marks didn't answer but leapt up, like a Prussian officer, offering his hand.

Zac didn't return the gesture, instead he beckoned a waitress, and ordered a pot of tea and some muffins.

Marks still hadn't offered an explanation, so he said,

"Before you start I've got some news for you."

"Last Friday there was an attempt to kidnap Kirsty outside her school, the police were called and they've been asking some awkward questions, but we managed to keep Lisa's disappearance a secret, Oh! and incidentally, they had Scottish accents too!" Zac explained.

"Good God! Marks muttered, obviously stunned. "How more serious can things become?"

"What's your news?" Zac queried.

"Well it was after I called around to see your good lady, Donna, I mean Mrs Gale, at your place, I thought I should make a few enquiries up at this end, I got in touch with a guy I know from my business days, at the Glasgow Herald, he agreed to search through some back editions for me, using the computer. And came up with some pretty rum stuff about our Mr McDonald,"

"Are you sure it's the same man Lisa met in Paris?" Zac asked.

Marks nodded, and went on,

"Apparently, back in ninety four, he was convicted of fraud down south, and sentenced to three years, he was released November ninety six, serving out the latter part of his time at Barlinnie prison, right here in Glasgow,"

"Surely they wouldn't have reported that locally would they?" Zac queried

"No, but his wife had created a fuss complaining it was too far for her to visit, using the paper to drum up support in order to have him transferred nearer home." Marks elaborated.

"How can you be so sure you got the same man, there must be thousands of McDonalds in and around Glasgow," Zac quizzed.

"Well like I told your good lady… I knew when I spotted him at Disney I'd seen him before, but the only thing that didn't tally was his blonde hair, I remembered when I first met him at a trade fair at Willesdon, he was dark and greying at the sides a little,"

"Right, but all this is yesterday's news, we still don't know where he is now," Zac said, getting impatient.

"My friend Duncan, went on to say he'd found another snippet on file from the Herald, this time from March ninety seven, it stated he'd been charged with evading excise duty on his car, giving a home address right here in the city, so I went over and checked it out," Marks went on.

Zac nodded.

"Over at Easterhouse, the same apartment block as the newspaper reported, but the guy I spoke to there said it was his apartment, and it had been for the last six years. He said I'd been mis-informed. When I told him I was making enquiries about a man called Hamish Mcdonald, he seemed to get angry and clamed up, telling me in no uncertain terms to clear off. Which I did, if you saw the size of him you'd understand why." Marks explained.

"The dates seem to add up, the caretaker at Hammersmith said he thought he was arrested around August ninety four, even if he had served a full three years, he'd have been out by then," Zac suggested.

"I got the impression he knew who I was talking about, instinct tells me he's back here on home ground, and has been since being released from prison, apart from a few forages down south now and then, those mail drops you talked about; he seems to move around a lot, that's why I asked you to come up here.

I know we don't exactly hit it off, but I think you'd agree our main priority is your sister. I suggest we split up and do a search, check anything and everything, police, courts, even surviving relatives, if there are any," Marks suggested.

"That's OK by me, but when this business is over, what I said before still goes, don't ever bother my sister unless she wants you to, understood?" Zac warned.

"OK I understand, what do you say to meeting here between four at five everyday, make it a base, I've got a room off Argyle Street, nearby. Have you got anything fixed up?" Marks questioned.

"Nothing yet, but I'll find somewhere," Zac said, adding.

"Why did you want to meet me in a tea room, why not a pub?"

"I didn't think you'd want to drink with me!" Marks said, getting up following Zac out on to the street.

Out of hear shot, Zac mumbled, 'You not wrong.'

It was a week to the day since being incarcerated in her small dingy cell, Lisa knew this, Hamish had brought in a radio, three days earlier.

Perhaps he had felt sorry for her, or, much more a probable, it was a sop to protect his investment.

Whatever! she knew for certain they wouldn't want a repeat of that crazy scenario last Tuesday, when she had managed to pin Maggi down on the floor, after the bitch had threatened if she didn't pay up, they would kidnap the kids too.

It took Hamish and the bruiser Broggi, nearly an hour to get some semblance of order into the tense situation, even gagging her, tying her hands and feet up again.

Maggi hadn't come near the room since.

Every morning, at the same time, Hamish accompanied her to the bathroom and Lisa used the time to get him talk more about himself and the situation they were in.

It was obvious he still liked her, but no matter what she said, she couldn't turn it to her advantage.

Whenever she thought she had succeeded in getting beneath his hard veneer, he would come over all philosophical and morose, saying it was his last real chance to get some big money.

Then yesterday afternoon, there was that kafuffle in the room next door.

Lisa distinctly heard Broggi say that someone had been around his place asking questions, enquiring about Hamish, who in turn denied knowing anything, most of the conversation was garbled, but the remark gave Lisa a ray of hope.

Was it the police? Was it Zac? Trying to find out where she had landed up.

Suddenly her train of thought was interrupted with a key scraping in the lock.

Hamish appeared,

"You seem to have got a friend, a knight on a white horse," he said, standing at the foot of her bed.

"What do you mean? I don't understand." Lisa replied, knowing he was about to question her.

"Some guy with a posh English accent, has been nosing around asking questions. Did you tell anyone you were going to Scotland?" he asked.

"Only my friend." she said.

"That must be it, he's been here asking some odd questions about my whereabouts."

"Your 'him' as you describe… is a she!" she sneered.

"Oh! Well maybe she told someone then, do you know him? He's tall with dark hair and a moustache."

Lisa, tried to disguise her surprise, replied, "Well I don't know anybody like that, d'you think I'd tell you even if I did, perhaps it was the police, have you thought of that? maybe they're on to you." Lisa said, enjoying the worried expression creeping across his face.

"We don't think it was, but if he, whoever he is, gets closer, you'll be on the move and you could end up out in a barn out in the sticks somewhere." he said.

"Do you really think so?" Lisa said, looking disdainfully around her prison like cell.," adding.

"What a pathetic lot you are, I hope it is the police, so they can put you behind bars again, kidnapping is just about as serious as you can get."

Hamish stamped noisily over to the door, opening it, he shouted.

"We ain't about to give up now, don't raise your hopes too much lady, or you are gonna be disappointed." Slamming the door, before he locked it.

Silence pervaded her dingy half lit room once more, lying on the dirty smelly mattress, she wondered if the white knight could indeed be Marks.

Beggars can't be chooser's, she thought, she would welcome even him, if he could extricate her from this hell, she found herself in.

As the long miserable day wore on she knew she had done the unthinkable, conceded to a hope, that it really was him. At the same time, Zac walked the city centre streets in search of bed and breakfast accommodation.

He found a room off Waterloo Street and literally threw his holdall on to a single bed, in the room, situated on the second floor.

Trying hard to heed the verbal warnings the landlady of the house gave him, before going out again.

But the lesson came home to him later. One thirty am, to be precise, one of the house rules must have been denial of access to his room in the wee small hours.

He'd been well and truly locked out.

A drinking session, and a chance meeting with an old lag friend from prison, Doodle McIntry, had caused his lateness.

There was nothing for it, but to make his way back to the multi-storey, to spend a cold shivery night bedded down across the back seats of the Frontera, covered by a flimsy car rug, that Lisa had fortuitously stored in the boot.

The heavens opened up as he left the tall concrete edifice the following morning, without the car, making sure he fed the meter.

He was making his way to the Registrar, on Martha Street for birth deaths, and marriages.

Doodle had given him the idea, relating a story about a old lag friend of theirs, who had found his long lost brother living here in the city, after checking the same source. Spending years, previously, on a wild goose chase, searching around every where.

Zac was thankful for the tip. The obvious wouldn't have crossed his mind, been too easy for him.

The trouble was, he didn't have a lot to go on, he remembered Lisa telling Donna that she was going to Coatbridge, a district east of the city. But the name McDonald must be as common as Smith is, south of the border.

He entered the Victorian building, adjoining the University of Strathclyde, and noticed the office was in stark contrast to another he had visited after his father had died, but.this one had a computer to facilitate searches,

After stating the nature of his visit, the sour- faced auburn head girl sitting at a desk, directed Zac to the computer screen, but only after a lot of uncertainty on her part, obviously wondering if he was a modern day tramp, his unkempt, unshaven appearance, dangerous in her hi- tech world.

She must have noticed he was having some difficulty with the mouse on the machine, and eventually came over to him, reluctantly giving up a few of minutes of her precious time, doling out some rudimentary instruction, but keeping him at arms length.

He soon discovered that this kind of search was only as good as any up to date information he had at hand, there were literally thousands of McDonald's living in and around the city, so he homed in on the Bargeddie and Coatbridge areas, seven or eight miles east of the city.

He managed to whittle the eighty or so names down to nine, with the same initials. Four of the number, being around the same age group as his quarry. All of who had lived in the Coatbridge area. But none of these names sported the Christian name of Hamish.

Making a note of these he made ready to leave the building but not before the same girl, made him aware of his appearance again, sniffing the air around him as she came near, then keeping him a full arm's length distance until she had guided him safely out of the door.

Before attempting to do anything else, he knew he had better mend his bridges with Nanette, his good landlady at Waterloo Street, he needed to retrieve his hold- all, so he could at least, have a wash and brush up.

It was still early so he decided after doing that, he would take a trip over to the Coatbridge area and check out some of the addresses, knowing the chances of most people still being there were slim, his hope was that someone there would remember. It was a long shot, but the only shot he had.

The landlady relented, but only after he had agreed to forfeit his first night's rent, earwigging him yet again, about the house rules.

Later, collecting the Frontier he found his way on to the busy Edinburgh road, and made for the district of Coatbridge.

Later that afternoon the two met at the tea rooms as planned, Marks ordered a pot of tea, a couple of wholemeal bread rolls, and some curious looking shortcake biscuits, before beginning to perform the ritual of pouring the tea and apportioning the snacks,

Zac looked on impatiently, waiting for his news.

"Well then?" he asked.

"No, you first," Marks suggested.

"I went over to the Registrar's office in Martha Street this morning, and got this list." he said, handing over a crumpled piece of paper.

"Good thinking… have you checked any of these out?" Marks quizzed.

"Two of them, one in Swinton Crescent, long gone, and another at Mitchell Street.

I'll do the other two tomorrow, there was nothing I could put my finger on there, so I called in a little corner shop at the end of another street.

The old lady there, called her husband out, from the backroom of the premises.

He said he had known the family, especially the father, Ian McDonald, deceased now, after working with him at the coal face in the old days. There were two boys, he said and a girl. He remembered the youngest boy was called Hamish, always in trouble with the law, and thought he'd moved away ages ago.

He asked me why I was looking for him. I told him he was a pal from my army days.

That figures, he said, the last time he saw Hamish was in Glasgow, in the company of an army man, the mercenary, Big Broggi Hamilton.

I asked him to give me a description, and he said, A huge guy, shaven headed and arms like a Gorilla, with strange snake-like of tattoo the back of his neck" Zac reported.

Marks looked shocked.

"What's the matter?" Zac asked, turning around, to see what was worrying him.

"That's the fellow I talked to at Easterhouse, a giant of a man, living at that address that Duncan gave me, he had a shaven head and tattoos too." Marks remembered.

Zac agreed with Marks that they should get over there and keep a close watch on the apartment; it was obvious he had lied.

"The old man at the shop was right, he said if you found Broggi, Hamish was bound to follow sooner or later, they seemed to be big pals," he said.

"If the big guy is connected, he's bound to be on his toes by now, especially since you already questioned him about his friend," Zac said.

"Well, let's put it this way, he's not the kind of bloke I'd choose to get on the wrong side of... but it looks like we have to." Marks concluded.

CHAPTER 10

At long last, their luck was in, the big man Broggi appeared from the front entrance of the building, and sauntered slowly over to a battered white, Transit van.

Glancing furtively up and down the street he jumped into the driving seat, then slammed the door, flicking the end of a lighted cigarette through the window, before revving the engine up, slowly moving off.

Zac was at the wheel of the Frontera, followed him at a discreet distance, down into Cournbrook Road, then left into Lochdochart, he seemed to be making his way into a country area.

It was drizzling and getting dark as they shadowed him, turning left on to the A752.

A quarter of an hour later they watched him as he pulled up outside a terraced house at the top end of Gerradie Street.

Concealing their vehicle behind a parked car, they watched closely as he opened the back doors of the van, taking out a cardboard box, and carrier bag.

A small woman, unmistakable in the yellow hue of a street lamp, opened the door and stepped aside to let him in, looking, up and down the street before closing the door.

Zac waited a few minutes, then ran down the street and checked the number of the house.

"Sixty Six!" he mumbled, as he dived back into the van, sinking down low into the driving seat.

"We have to get into that house somehow," Marks said.

"I doubt if that's possible, not tonight anyway, look! we know where the big man resides now, we got the number of this house, what do you say we leave things 'till tomorrow, I don't think they are gonna do a runner just yet," Zac suggested.

"You're probably right, perhaps we'll get a good night's kip now we know what the situation is, I don't think I've slept more than two hours at a stretch since we started this caper." said Marks, yawning.

Six am sharp, the following morning, Zac called around to Hope Street to collect his unlikely partner.

He had managed to borrow a set of aluminium extension ladders from Nanette, the landlady at Waterloo Street, and had secured them to his roof rack, tying a red rag to the rear end, to serve as a warning flag.

Marks appeared through the door looking absolutely ridiculous with a woollen hat pulled tightly over his head covering his ears; obviously thinking he was taking part in some clandestine mission.

"Did you get the coveralls and that?" Zac asked.

"Yes in here!" he said, pointing to the bulky carrier bag he was holding.

"Let's go then," Zac said, manoeuvring out on to the road.

The journey to Coatbridge, seemed shorter than before, they followed the same route but the roads were relatively empty, this early in the morning,

They parked up between two cars, further on down the road this time, now that it was light.

"What's to do?" Marks enquired.

"First things first, what d'you say to some breakfast," Zac said, leaning over to the back seat, grabbing at a Thermos flask and package, covered in silver foil.

"Nanette, gave me these too, made it up for me, she thinks I work as a building contractor," he said grinning, unwrapping the package, handing Marks a squashed toasted egg sandwich.

Two and a half long, tedious hours ticked by and Marks complained his long legs were starting to give him cramp, but Zac warned him not get out of the car, reminding him they had already seen his face.

No sooner had they settled down again, when Zac blurted out.

"I think I've spotted our man,"

Marks, who couldn't see anything from his side, asked if he meant Hamish or the big man.

"Our mystery man Hamish! I think, he's about the same height as you, with darkish hair, he looks a lot like you in fact," he replied.

"I've got to see this," he said, opening his door, pretending to adjust the windscreen wiper.

He soon collapsed back onto his seat, shouting excitedly.

"That's him alright, he was the one with Lisa in Paris,"

A short time later the big man Broggi came out, stepping backwards, as if talking to someone in the doorway.

Turning quickly, he jumped into the driving side and they made off down the street at some speed.

"He must have stayed the night, our luck is in, they're off somewhere," Zac muttered, as if talking aloud to himself.

"What's the plan then?" Marks asked.

"You say you got everything in that bag, we'll change into the overalls, take the bucket, then knock at the door, we'll act like a couple of window cleaners touting for work, but don't forget, try to mimic the accent, otherwise she'll get suspicious right away.

I'll follow a couple of minutes later with the ladders over my shoulder," Zac explained.

"What do we do then?" Marks asked, listening intently.

"Play it by ear, I hope she plays along but I'll use the ladder as a wedge, if she try's to slam the door on us," Zac explained.

"What if the men come back unexpectedly?" Marks asked.

"We can't plan for that, cross your fingers and pray they don't." Zac replied.

By the time Marks had buttoned his overalls up to his neck and pulled his woollen cap down over his ears again, Zac couldn't help but think the man had just crawled out of a long forgotten history book, appearing like some medieval artisan.

He jumped out of the Frontera and crossed to the other side of the street, then ambled quietly down to number sixty-six.

He knocked on the door, and waited.

Seconds later it opened up a couple of inches, coming to stop on a safety chain, and the side of a woman's face appeared.

"Yes?" she asked.

"My pal and me are looking for work window cleaning. D'you need anything done?" he asked.

"We do our own," she mumbled, inspecting him from his head down to his boots.

"Les! I've got the ladders, does the lady want them cleaned?" Zac shouted, dramatically. The ladders coming into her field of vision before he did

Curious, she kept the door open a second or two longer until their eyes met.

Zac smiled, then quickly turned on heel, sweeping the ladders around ninety degrees, the door had just about closed, but Zac marched forward and butted the end of the ladders into it, forcing it open, the momentum crashing the door noisily against the inside wall.

Dropping the ladders he lunged forward and caught her by the shoulders, trying his best to restrain her from getting away.

Marks suddenly loomed up from behind and cupped her mouth with his hand, managing to stop her yelling out.

After the commotion had died down a little, Zac dashed into the front room that overlooked the street, in order to observe the activity, just in case someone had heard all the excitement.

Satisfied, there wasn't any reaction, he came back and grabbed the curtain rail from the little hall window, and ripped the drape into lengths, gagging the woman, and tying her hands behind her back.

Fixing his eyes firmly on hers, he said, menacingly.

"Where's Lisa?"

The woman, her blue eyes wide with fear above the gag, nodded her head from side to side.

"I'll ask you once more, where is Lisa? you know who I'm talking about... where is she?" Zac ordered, shouting louder now.

Maggi's eyelids closed, as she collapsed forward from the waist down, sinking to the bottom of the stair- well, muttering something inaudible from beneath the gag.

"Remove the gag." Zac ordered.

"Say it again woman," he commanded the frightened woman.

"She's upstairs...inside the box room."

Zac literally flew up the narrow staircase two steps at a time, reaching the landing he pushed open a door that was already ajar on his left, realizing it was a large double bedroom, he sprinted on further to a door at the end of the landing.

It was locked.

In his excitement he didn't think about a key, instead he rushed at it like a demented Rhino, and on the second attempt managed to crash it open, revealing a sparsely furnished room, with a single bed.

Returning on to the landing he shouted angrily.

"Bring her up Phil,"

The tall man literally lifted Maggi up into his arms and carried her to the top of the stairs like a child, placing her feet vertically on the landing as soon as he reached the top.

"You said the box room, there's no one here, you'd better stop playing charades woman, we know she's here somewhere in this house," he raged.

Marks removed the gag again.

"Now show me," Zac ordered.

Maggi entered and went over to the wardrobe at the side of the bed, and began pushing it with her shoulder towards the window.

Zac joined her and they soon realized it had been concealing a door.

This one too, was locked. Maggi turned around quickly saying she'd get the key.

"Oh! no you don't my lady, stay exactly where you are," Zac said bracing himself, then barged at it with his shoulder.

It took three attempts, this time the door splintered into a half dozen jagged pieces.

"Keep an eye on her Phil, make sure she doesn't make a run for it," Zac ordered, as he took a tentative step forward into the dingy, dim- lit room.

To his left he saw the steel base of another bed, and tied to this were someone's feet…bare feet, he took another step forward, and realized he had found his sister, her hands covering her face, but there was no mistake, It was his sister alright.

"Oh! God Zac, it is you… isn't it." She sobbed.

"It's me love, what have the barstards done to you," he said, reaching down to hold her.

Her relief was obvious as he hugged her

Marks, secured Maggi's hands behind her back and took her into the main bedroom, and tied her to the radiator.

Returning to the box room he stood just behind the open door and looked down at Lisa.

He wanted to be the one to console her, hug her, but she didn't even know he was there.

What would her reaction be when she did. He thought

He stepped further back behind the door, as if by doing so, he could keep the situation neutral.

Zac's voice boomed out.

"Phil come in here will you." Hesitating, he took a step forward.

"Hello! Lisa." He said.

"So you was that bloody knight after all," she muttered, her face contorted with anger instead of relief.

"What was that?" her brother asked, standing now, undoing the rope around her feet.

"Oh it doesn't matter, I'm gobsmacked that's all," She said, painfully dragging her legs over, to sit on the edge of the bed.

Suddenly, her anger became a hysterical vocal tirade.

"What the hell are you doing here," She shouted, giving him no chance to respond.

"We wouldn't have found you without his help Sis... Philip realized when he was at Disney land that he had seen the Scotsman before, and it went on from there!" Zac explained.

"So it was you at that holiday camp, frightening the kids, how is it you to pop up in every little episode of my life.... even this one," Lisa screamed, covering her face with her hands, and sobbing again.

Marks glanced at Zac, and without saying anything, and walked quietly away.

Zac led his sister to the bathroom, then found Marks in the main bedroom overlooking the street.

"We have to report this to the police," he said, still looking straight ahead.

"I suppose so," Zac agreed, then elaborated.

"We've been so busy we didn't plan this part, but I'm gonna suggest something different...something I know you won't agree with, I suggest we do nothing...nothing at all, warn the woman, but leave it there. Lisa can't face anymore hassle, it would crack her up if she has to attend court after all that's happened,"

"I feel for Lisa too, but do you honestly think they will forget this, well do you?" Marks reasoned.

"They'll be too frightened to take it any further, they know if they did the police would get involved,"

"No! We have to finish this once and for all, I'm going to ring them right now or Lisa will be haunted by this for the rest of her life," he said, firmly, stepping quickly over to the phone in the hall.

All Zac could hear was a short, sharp one-sided conversation, before the phone was slammed down noisily.

"The police are on their way," Marks said, abruptly.

Zac went upstairs and told Lisa what was happening, then went into the front bedroom to check on Maggi, who, by this time was on her knees on the floor, her arms tied behind her, with a longer rope secured to the radiator pipes.

Surveying the street below, Zac had visions of half a dozen police cars screeching around the corner, lights flashing and sirens wailing, but like so many real life situations, the opposite was the case.

A panda car, and a van, glided silently around the corner, coming to a halt opposite the front door.Marks, already downstairs peering through the front room window, went to the door to meet them.

Two men, one in plain clothes, the other uniformed displaying the three stripes of a Sergeant, followed him inside the house.

Zac guided Lisa downstairs.

"So you're the lady." The sergeant said, by way of a greeting, adding.

"I'm Sergeant Robson from the Strathclyde division, Mr Marks here has kindly sketched in a few details, would you be kind enough as to sit down here," he said, leading her to the settee in the front room.

"Put the fire on Alex the lady is shivering," The sergeant ordered.

The plain-clothes man, who seemed somewhat short for a policeman, nodded, then bent over to click the ignition, transforming the cold sparse room, into a place of flickering shadows.

Marks, meanwhile went up stairs and brought Maggi down to the same room.

"I know you don't I." the plain-clothes man remarked, staring intently at her,

"Met you in court about eighteen months ago, you're Hamish McDonald's wife, aren't you?"

Maggi looked down to the floor, not attempting to answer.

"Take her out to the van Alex please, we'll question her at the station." Robson instructed.

Lisa, went on to explain how she met Hamish at Disneyland in Paris, explaining how he had befriended her and the kids, and then went on to paint a picture about her unexpected confinement, and the cruel treatment she had received over the ten days.

"What do you think their motive was for keeping you here?" he queried.

Lisa hesitated, "Well I...er.. told him I had changed my mind about him, and wanted to go home." she said, trying hard not to mention anything about her lottery win.

The sergeant paused for a while, as if trying to take it all in.

Getting up, he asked them to excuse him for a minute or two, so he could move the vehicles, in case the men came back.

A few minutes later he marched back in and took up the same seat.

"Did you come up on your own volition or by invitation?" he asked.

"A bit of both really, he told me I could visit him anytime I liked." she replied.

"I ask that, because this will be the bone of contention, I must know if you asked to come up here. You see looking in from the outside, your case seems cut and dried, but looking from inside out, so to speak, it's not nearly so strong." he explained.

"Yes I think I understand." Lisa replied.

"Well, it's obvious, they are going to deny they took you prisoner, I know how these men work, they will say you stayed here because you wanted to, 'cos… if you don't mind me saying, you had taken a fancy to this Hamish fellow.

Lisa broke down into a flood of tears again, as Zac sat her down, resting her head upon his chest.

"Don't you think she's suffered enough already man, she's not ready for all this yet." Marks butted in.

The front door slammed shut and the detective Ferguson, clumped noisily up the staircase.

A second or two later he shouted down from the top of the stairs.

"Blue Transit coming up the street."

"That sounds like them." Zac shouted, leaping up from the settee and diving over to side of the window.

"That's them alright." he confirmed.

Sergeant Robson grabbed at Lisa's wrist and dragged her unceremoniously into the hallway, instructing her to go upstairs.

"Alex get down here quick." He ordered, then turning to Zac and Marks he said.

"You two keep out of the way somewhere, until we have confronted them.

Hamish let himself in with his key, but the big man wasn't with him.

Shouting out for his wife a number of times, he walked into the living room.

Alex and Robson, crouched low in a cupboard beneath the stairs, but realized they had a dilemma.

They had seen Hamish come in, through the gap at the door, but where was the big man?

Still out in the van perhaps? was he about to come in?

They had to make a decision, and quickly!

"Let's take our chances." Robson whispered, nudging his colleague.

Crashing out of the hideaway they caught up with Hamish just as he was about to climb the stairs, they grabbed his arms and wrestled him to his knees, then forced his arms up behind his back, quickly handcuffing him.

Hamish had been caught completely by surprise.

"Who the bloody hell are you when you're at home?" he grunted.

"Look closer man, and you'll probably know us." Robson mumbled, still breathless.

"I'm Sergeant Robson and this Detective Constable Alex Ferguson from the Strathclyde division, and we're arresting you on suspicion of kidnapping."

"Where's your pal Broggi Hamilton." Alex butted in.

"Pal! I've got no pal, if you think I've got one you look for him. Pal," Hamish sneered sarcastically.

"Take him out to the van Alex, let him join his wife," Robson ordered.

Then turning to Lisa he said.

"As soon as the forensic squad arrives I'd like you to check in at the Western Infirmary to make sure there's no personal injury… for your own sake, and our evidence of course, then I'd like you all to meet me at the station later, to make a written statement."

As soon as the squad had finished, Zac agreed to accompany Lisa to the hospital in the police van.

Marks, meanwhile drove Zac's van back to the city and booked some rooms at the Carrick Hotel, in the city centre.

The two men had argued to go back home immediately, but Lisa wanted to stay over night to calm down and recuperate for a while, to get her head together before picking up the children at Barbara's.

The medical check up complete, and photographs taken of her bruises left by the rope marks on her arms and legs, they were taken back to the police station to make their statements.

Robson was already there.

"Why did you lie to me about their reasons for kidnapping you Mrs Whittle?" he asked, as soon as she sat down.

"I just didn't want money to be the real reason for it." Lisa said, realizing by now how naïve she'd been, it was obvious that Maggi and Hamish, would talk after being questioned.

CHAPTER 11

Sitting alongside Zac, driving the Frontera, Lisa wasn't unduly worried about returning home to Pennington. Nothing could be as bad as the last two weeks of hell she had lived through, being a lottery winner paled by comparison.

Philip Marks too, had surprised her, the hate she'd once had for him, had turned into a kind of sneaking respect. She was aware that had it not been for his interest in her, albeit an obsessional one, she'd still be incarcerated in that hell- hole.

Not everything in the garden was rosy however, the Sergeant warned them the big man Broggi had got away, and was still at large. But surely a man with his grotesque appearance shouldn't be too hard to spot. Lisa thought, seeking reason for assurance.

Anyway, first stop Altringham; to pick up the kids, the thought threatened to choke her with emotion, she could hardly wait to see them, ordering her brother to put his foot down. Zac thumped the horn as soon as they pulled up outside Barbara's house, at eighteen Cherry grove Avenue.

The kids mobbed her as soon as she left the car, Kirsty leapt up on her, wrapping her legs around he waist, Ben was crying and tugging at her skirt, and mixed in the middle, was Barbara, smothering her with kisses.

Barbara and Eric seemed concerned about her appearance, saying she looked pale and drawn, as they went into the house

"Been burning the candles at both ends, have you?" Eric said.

"No, I've got a lot to tell you, and got some apologizing to do too, I went up to Scotland to meet a man I got friendly with, when the kids and I went on holiday to Disneyland in Paris, but the whole episode turned very nasty." Lisa explained.

"C'mon now, tell them truth Sis, she was kidnapped!" Zac said, butting in.

"Good heavens! Is this true?" Barbara asked, leaving her chair to sit down next to her.

"The man was part of an organized gang of villains, it was like something out of a black comedy... they even tried to kidnap Kirsty on the way home from school, that's why Zac brought them up here." Lisa explained.

"We didn't say anything at the time, because we weren't absolutely sure about it, there wasn't any demand note or anything, so we couldn't be sure what they were up to, until some of their associates tried to abduct Kirsty." Zac elaborated.

"Why would they want to kidnap you and the kids?" Eric asked.

"I was going to tell you in time but I won a great deal of money on the lottery, and that I could live the normal life, I was mistaken, "Lisa said.

There was shocked silence, until Barbara broke the spell, blurting,

"Well some of the people I've read about seem to manage it."

"The police, what about the police, they know don't they?" Eric interjected.

"Oh! Yes." Zac said, taking Eric's elbow and leading him out into the garden to explain about the course of events.

Barbara volunteered to have the children a few more days, so she could sort out her affairs, but Lisa was adamant she'd never leave them again.

Zac was itching to get back home to Donna, he had phoned her almost everyday since being away, and could tell she was at her wits end trying to and run the shop alone, not knowing what had become of everyone she cared for.

Just over an hour and a quarter later they turned into Cashmere Avenue; Donna was already at the front door waiting for them.

"Thank heavens you're home free, I thought I'd lost you, Zac told me all about it, he tells me that one of the bastard's is still at large, is that right?" she said, taking her hand and leading her into the lounge.

Zac made a beeline for the kitchen, grabbing a can of lager from the fridge, gulping from it without a glass as he returned to the living room.

"Leave her alone Donna love, she's just been through I don't know how many post mortems at Mum's." he said, collapsing into a chair and placing his feet up on the coffee table.

"Oh! By the way Marks rang about an hour ago, asked if you'd arrived home yet." Donna said, changing the subject.

"That was quick Sis, you only saw him this morning, the poor man seems lost without you." Zac said, grinning.

"That's not funny Zac, the last thing I want now is him getting back to the way he was before." Lisa snapped back.

"Well I got to know him up there in Scotland, and he turned out better than I imagined he'd be." He said.

"My opinion hasn't changed, you're not a woman you don't see the things we do, right Donna." Lisa said, trying to solicit her friend's support.

"That's as maybe, but if wasn't for him we'd still be searching the country for you." Zac said.

"If you are worried about thanking him, don't worry, I will one of these days, but a verbal thank you only, and that's as far as it goes." Lisa said, adamantly.

Donna, who hadn't said much up until then, spoke out.

"You'll need to watch him more now, you're a lady of means remember, perhaps he's looking to be paid for his troubles."

"Don't worry he won't get a penny off me, I can't forget how he treated Martyn." Lisa said.

Kirsty was getting fidgety by this time and asked to go home. Ben was out to the world, sleeping on the settee.

"I checked the house this morning everything seems OK, there hasn't been a sign of the reporters for over a week now, so I think it's safe." Donna said.

Lisa collected her coat from the hallstand, and Zac carried Ben out to the car.

"You know, I wouldn't care if those damn news hounds were there, I'd give them their interview and poke two fingers up to them and the world, everybody in Penington must know who I am by now anyway… Sod them." she shouted, driving off.

All was quiet in the close as she unlocked the front door, having some difficulty opening it. A stack of assorted mail had literally cluttered up the doorway.

Kirsty offered to put the kettle on to make a cup of coffee as Lisa laid her sleeping son on the settee.

It was great to be back, she thought, she wasn't even going to attempt to sort the mail out, most of it was junk anyway, and the rest, probably heart rendering begging letters, usually coming as they did, in little white envelopes with the neat joined up writing.

She'd get Zac to sort them, see if there was anything worthy of a bob or two.

Lisa didn't care anymore, if the worst came to the worst she would move, far away from

Pennington altogether.

Her thoughts were interrupted with the trill of the phone.

Lifting the receiver up, she asked who was calling, but there was dead silence at the other end, she didn't wait for the tell tale click of a receiver being returned, she slammed hers down first.

Tears welled up in her eyes again, Kirsty ran over trying to console her.

"What is it Mummy?" she asked starting to cry herself.

Her voice, hardly discernible through a barrage of emotion, cried.

"If this is what winning the lottery means, I wish I had the power to put the clock back."

Kirsty cried along with her mother, then Ben added his voice to the chorus, crying too.

Pulling herself together, she undressed him and carried him upstairs to bed.

Surely Marks wouldn't try all that idiotic nonsense again, she thought, even he couldn't be that stupid.

Guilt seem to envelope her yet again, perhaps she had shown too much gratitude, making him think he had carte blanche to play his silly games again, maybe...just maybe it wasn't him at all, she'd been wrong before, twice in fact.

She'd have to enlist Zac's help again.

The following Monday, with the children back at school, she went into town and back to work in the shop for the day.

It was good to pretend that nothing had changed. Donna acted like she always had, not spoiling things, asking questions about the future and what it might hold.

And she reciprocated, not mentioning anything about the mysterious phone calls.

By Wednesday she was beginning to feel confident again, so she left Donna at the shop, to walk to the town centre, to do some shopping. Ever since she had arrived back, she dreaded the thought of people stopping her, enquiring about her good fortune, but thankfully no one ever did.

Everything seemed normal and boringly mundane, until she left Barratts, the chemist shop, it was then that she came to a dead stop. Just for an instant, shivers coursed up and down her spine leaving goose pimples on the back of her neck

Surely it can't be him, she thought, she had seen him everyday for ten days, but always in the shadows of that dimly lit room, anyway, she reasoned, his patch was up north not down here in Pennington, he wouldn't come this far south…. would he?

She started to walk again, trying to connect the phone calls, she started to walk faster still, knowing that she had to talk to someone about it, and quick!

Donna was rearranging the shop window when she entered.

"What's the matter, you look as if you've seen a ghost," her friend asked, noting how strained she looked.

"I think my mind is beginning to playing tricks on me." she said, letting her shopping bag slide to the floor.

"What d'you mean?" Donna asked.

"I think I saw Broggi Hamilton of all people on the corner of Healy and Barratts, the dry cleaners."

"Did you have a good look at him?" her friend asked.

"No, only from the back, the shaven head and tattoo, with that horrible snake on his neck. It really gave me the shivers " Lisa replied.

"Oh! that's nothing unusual these days, lot's of people have them, I expect it was just someone that looked like him." Donna said, trying to reassure her.

"And the phone calls, what about them." Lisa said.

"What phone calls?" Donna quizzed again.

"When I first arrived back home, I picked up the receiver, but there was no one at the other end, the second one was on the answering machine, with horrible heavy breathing that time." Lisa explained.

After a lot of persuasion Lisa conceded it may have been a case of mistaken identity, Donna Marie gave her an example of something she had experienced recently, talking to a woman for over an hour thinking she was an old school friend, then realising she wasn't, after they had both relived years at a secondary school.

She raised a smile on her friend's face when she concluded she hadn't let on, but the woman, whose name she still didn't know, regularly relived the experience whenever she bumped into her in town.

Lisa agreed to forget it for the time being, but there were a couple of conditions.

The first, to let Sergeant Robson know, and tell him what she thought she saw. The other, was that Donna and Zac to promise they would stay over at her place for a couple of nights until she felt safe again.

On the Friday morning the detective Ferguson turned up at the shop.

Sergeant Robson and himself had come down from Glasgow to clarify their statements and check out Lisa's supposed sighting of Broggi Hamilton.

He wanted all of them up at Penington Central police station at two p.m. that afternoon.

Zac drove her there, and as soon as they entered the young policeman on duty kept staring at her.

"I know you don't I? You're that woman who scooped the lottery, saw your picture in the Courier." he said, with a knowing grin.

Lisa didn't answer.

"Look, little boy blue, we're here on business to see Sergeant Robson, do you mind, where is he? Zac quipped.

"He's waiting for you in that room over there." he said, still grinning, pointing to the first of two doors on the right of the corridor.

The two familiar Scottish policemen greeted them as they entered the office.

But it wasn't until they sat down in front of the dour Sergeant, that they realised no one had thought of telling Philip Marks about the interview.

Ferguson volunteered to drive over to the Drayton Manor estate to get him.

"The big man is still at large then?" Zac asked.

"I'm afraid so, but I'm not to sure that he's down here." Robson replied.

"I could have sworn it was him, but I realised afterwards I only saw him from the rear, so I'm not so sure now." Lisa said.

Just then a double rap sounded at the door.

The same young policeman that had been on the desk, pushed sideways through the door, carrying a tray with a pot of tea, cups, saucers and accruements upon it.

"Where's Ferguson then?" he asked, eyeing up the situation in the room.

"He'll be back shortly, thank you constable, that's all." the Sergeant said, passing the tea around. The young policeman walked back to the door in slow motion, still staring and grinning at Lisa.

"Big Broggi Hamilton has been know to us for the last twelve years or more, I've never known him to operate south of Glasgow before, but before he came to our attention, he served as a mercenary...A soldier of fortune so I've been told, so I've warned your Inspector Gutteridge here, to keep a beady eye out for him just in case he does wander south" Robson explained.

There was another knock on the door, this time Philip Marks entered, closely followed by the Detective Constable.

"Alec here tells me you thought you saw Big Broggi Hamilton?" he said.

"I thought I had, but I'm not so sure now." Lisa replied.

"Why didn't you tell me?" Marks asked.

"You've done enough, there's no need for you to bother anymore, anyway it's in police hands now." Zac said, trying to save his Sister further explanations.

"Has McDonald and his wife been charged yet?" Marks probed.

"Yes they're on remand, the next hearing at the Sheriff's court in Paisley, we're hoping we'll have Hamilton by then." Ferguson cut in.

"Will we have to make an appearance in court then?" Zac asked.

"Yes, but don't worry, it won't be for a time yet, I'll let you know when, Oh! by the way Mrs Whittle, what made you think that man was Hamilton?" The Sergeant said, opening his briefcase, and spreading their statements on the table in front of them.

"The tattoo on the side of his neck, a snake curled 'round a stick." Lisa explained.

"Are you sure it wasn't something else?" he asked.

"Well I'm not too sure now." she replied.

"I'd like you all to be patient and go through this with me again, this time Mrs Whittle, please state why you think they kidnapped you, the lottery stuff is your business, but the motive for this crime is mine."

It had gone three pm by the time they finished, and the young constable still grinned as they passed the desk.

"How about a contribution for our Christmas fund then?" he asked, holding his hand out to Lisa.

Zac tossed him a fifty pence piece, saying,

"Stick that in your Christmas fund, buy some orange juice for the boys."

Lisa took the wheel on the way back, and dropped Zac off at Donna's house, then drove straight to the nursery and primary schools to pick up the kids.

The school didn't much like her picking them up early, and she found herself inventing excuses in each case for being premature, but she really needed their company.

Turning the key in the front door lock, she had a feeling of despair again.

Donna and Zac had spent the last two nights at the house, and even though she had the children she felt lonely, it was the same thing every night, getting the kids off to sleep then drowning her emotions in Vodka and Lemonade.

Even Pam her next door neighbour had surprised her by not coming around for her weekly chats, she probably thought it would be mis-interpreted as personal gain or something. She had heard of situations like this before, but didn't really believe it, yet people she had considered good friends, simply didn't bother anymore, all of them keeping their distance

Perhaps, it was all the excitement she had experienced these last months, all that adrenaline pumping around in her veins, whatever the reason, she was really missing Martyn, and missing those meaningful hungry years they had shared together.

Time heals, people said, but for her it seemed only to intensify feelings of loneliness. Fear too, seemed to be taking it's toll in her life, she'd never been one to run away from life's problems, but events were piling up one upon another, leaving her no time to think things through. She longed for somebody she could share her troubles with.

She had only just got Kirsty off to sleep, when somebody knocked the front door. Whoever the caller was, it was someone tall, the outline of the head and shoulders well above the rose motif on the opaque glass in the door. Her heart raced as she opened it. It was Philip Marks.

"Hope you don't mind me calling around Lisa, but I had to come around, for what it's worth, I think it was Hamilton you saw, and I knew I had to warn you or I'd never forgive myself." he said.

"Why do you say that?" Lisa asked, still unsure about letting him in.

"It was something Robson said, about the tattoo, not many people have got those things on their neck… and don't you think it suspicious that they came down so soon after your report."

Her fears were rekindled, as she invited him inside.

I must be off my trolley asking him in, she thought, as he sat down on the settee.

"I had a private word with Ferguson afterwards, and it was his opinion he could be down here, because unlike what Robson had said, records show he'd been down south many times in the past." Marks said.

Now was her chance, Lisa thought.

"Have you made any funny phone calls lately?" she probed.

"I don't know what you mean." he said, looking puzzled.

"I've had two since returning from Scotland, and if I thought for one minute you were responsible, I'd let Zac loose on you." she said.

"What can I say… hand on heart it wasn't me, can't you see that's just what I've been talking about, it was probably Hamilton, or one of his gang checking up on you." he said.

"Well that's as maybe, but there are a few thing we have to get straight,

I hated you and I think I still do, yet I'm thankful for what you've done, but can't you see… I'm scared, even at this moment, to say it." Lisa said.

"Why?" Marks asked, with a naive expression on his face.

"Because of the crazy way you acted before, the way you've always been, don't you understand I'm a woman, and you've haunted me with your crazy obsession, don't you see, you were responsible for my husbands death, albeit, indirectly.

No! I hate you with a vengeance, but I know I have to thank you for helping me." she said, tears welling up in her eyes.

"There's no need." Marks mumbled.

"I want you to promise me, after tonight you will keep well out of my life, do you understand?" Lisa said firmly.

"I can't." he said, grabbing her wrist.

"I love you and I always will, 'till my dying breath." he said, loudly.

Every instinct told Lisa to pull her arm away, but something made her freeze, it wasn't fear or loss of reason, but a strange kind of peace that felt right.

Even when he started to undo the buttons on her blouse she made no attempt to remove her hand from his vice like grip.

Her wrist pained when he let go, and hurt even more, as she helped him remove the rest of her clothing, she needed freedom and longed for it, not the kind to fly away, but the freedom to spend herself in an orgy of emotion, to confront and rid herself of all the ghosts that had haunted her for so very long.

Marks got up and walked over to the light switch, turning it off.

His shadow, as if on stilts, following him across the wall until they merged.

Lisa knew this wasn't going to be easy, her emotions were in turmoil, her heart thumped faster, as she instinctively raised her hand and slapped his face, then, turning it, drew back again and slapped him, with even more force, with the back of her hand, the opposite side.

"You are a male whore, d'you understand, a whore, you have nothing to offer, no pride, no respect, nothing just base animal instincts."

Marks tightened his grip on the nape of her neck, and with his free hand, pushed her gently down, on to the rug in front of the fire.

Moaning, she looked up as he bent down and kissed her, the sound of his heavy breathing drowning out the hum of gas feeding a flickering rainbow of flames, casting shadows around them.

Closing her eyelids, she could still discern the short sharp changes of light as he gripped her hips with heavy hands, dragging her expectant body towards him.

Her cries weren't songs of surrender, instead the wails of one about to be exorcised of demons, as she was capitulated, into a dark unknown universe.

"I love you, I love you, I always have and you know it, can't you see we are destined for each other.?" he moaned, as he rose up above her.

Lisa grabbed his hair with her two hands, and pulled his head down upon her chest, then rolled over, taking him with her.

Her hands still gripped his hair as she raised his head up, then banged it down upon the rug several times, shouting,

"I hate you still you bastard, you know why don't you… don't you!" she screamed, clawing his face, until the tears of pain and mental anguish, quickly extinguished his desire forcing him in a wasteland of emptiness.

Marks, shocked with her venom, tried to free himself from under, but she lay heavily upon him, riding him and slapping him, until he gave himself up into a fog of frenzy.

There was no remorse, Lisa knew in her heart if she was put in the same position; the same scenario would be re-enacted again. Everything that had happened was the exact opposite of what anyone, and more importantly she, would have predicted. Good had become evil, and light- darkness, sucking her into the irresistible black hole, that fate had carved out for her. It was her catharsis.

She felt as Faust must have felt when he had mortgaged his soul to the devil.

But there wasn't a winner or loser in this hell, nothing had turned out like they had envisaged.

She was free of all her demons that had haunted her for so long.

He, hurt, raped by the sceptres of hate, revenge and vindictiveness, demoralized now, becoming the hunted, not the hunter.

Now, at least they were equal, there was no going back, she had nothing to re-approach herself for.

Now what? Lisa mused, the once proud Marks, had taken off, without a word, soon after their encounter, reinforcing her belief that she had won the day.

She would call the tune from now on, she thought, swallowing the remains of her drink in the glass.

Switching the light on up at the landing, she climbed the stairs, wearing a contented smile.

Knowing from that moment on, she was free now… free to be free.

CHAPTER 12

The next morning Lisa was up early, feeling as if a heavy load had been lifted off her shoulders, she felt happier, younger even, the fog of worry had dissipated.

She wanted to plan for the future, explore her options; that her newly acquired wealth afforded her.

First things first though, she mused, deciding to do her bit at the shop, Her friend Donna deserved a break having done more than her fair share these last months.

Feeling unusually benevolent, she decided to drop the children off at school earlier than usual, then double back, open up the shop, and surprise her friend before she arrived.

Her fiend Donna Marie was curious, seeing her there with her light blue coverall already on.

"Had some kind of nervous breakdown have you?" she asked.

"Thought I'd surprise you, give you a break, God knows you deserve it," Lisa replied.

"Talking about surprises, I've got one for you," her friend said.

" Well c'mon don't keep me in suspense, you're always stealing my thunder anyway, what is it?" Lisa asked, intrigued.

"I'm gonna take the plunge with Zac," she exclaimed.

"When did you decide this?" Lisa asked.

"Well strictly speaking, we haven't, at least Zac hasn't, he doesn't know anything about it yet," she elaborated.

"I take it he will," Lisa suggested.

"When I'm good and ready," she promised.

"That's absolutely wonderful, I've been wanting to talk to you, to thank you for everything you've done these last few months, I've got a proposal for you too." Lisa said.

"What's that?" Donna asked.

"What do you say to you and Zac moving in with me, permanently?" Lisa suggested.

Her friend didn't say anything, and she went on,

"Until I make other arrangements that is," she explained.

"That sounds ominous," Donna quipped, eager to know the rest.

"I'm thinking of moving from this nosy old town altogether, start a new life somewhere else," Lisa elaborated.

"Why?" her friend, asked again.

"Too many awful memories for one, but if you agree, the house and shop will become yours, what d'you say?" she said.

"What can I say, that would be a fantastic wedding present... for my part I'd give you the thumbs up now, but I'll have to have a word with you know who first." she said, leaning over and giving her friend a peck on her cheek.

That evening Zac and Donna turned up on her doorstep, with two bulging suitcases.

"If you ask me he's the original opportunist, he's agreed to this and accepted my proposal all in the space of an hour," Donna said, greeting Lisa and lugging the case, following him through the hall.

Zac dumped his case in the kitchenette, and shouted.

"What about the house in Cashmere Avenue, shall we put the sale boards up?"

"It's early days yet, but I can't see any reason why not...what kind of mortgage have you got on it love?" she shouted to Donna, not knowing where she disappeared to.

"Seventeen or eighteen thou I think, it's on an endowment policy. I haven't looked since Oliver done a flit," she shouted from the lounge.

"We'll talk bout that nearer your big day, have you fixed a date yet?" Lisa probed.

"No! we've talked about everything but that, don't worry he won't miss the big day not with everything you've offered," her friend replied.

"What was that?" Zac asked, tugging at the ring from a can of lager he'd found in the fridge.

"Nothing to concern you, keep your pecker out bro, this is woman's business, right Lise," she said. Oh! And Zac, has Donna here spelt out my conditions?" Lisa asked, winking at her friend.

"No, she never said anything to me," he said, looking puzzled.

"Get rid of that heap of junk you call a van, I don't want people thinking I have rented a rooms to a couple of new- age travelers," she said.

Nothing was said about the wedding after that, but Lisa deduced it wouldn't be long, not if the frequency of her friend's shopping forages had anything to do with it, as well as her stepbrother permanently holding fort bric-a-brac.

"A week tomorrow at the registrar office in town."

"No church wedding then?" Lisa questioned.

"Zac wants to keep it low profile, he's still out on parole you know," she explained.

"Oh! Yes, I'd completely forgotten that, they can't stop him getting hitched…can they?" Lisa said, somewhat bewildered.

"No! But dumbo here, has invited his old probation officer to be our best man, he lives down here now. It's his way of showing the world he's turned over a new leaf," Donna explained.

"Well if it wasn't him… whatever his name is, it would have to be some other stranger, all his best friends are still inside." she chuckled.

Lisa was pleased with the way the children were settling down again, they thought it exciting their Uncle and Aunty were living under the same roof as them, and it wasn't surprising really, little Ben had acquired a permanent playmate and regular bedtime story teller.

But Kirsty let it be known in no uncertain terms, that she was disappointed with the wedding, she had set her heart on being a bridesmaid.

It took a lot of explaining that there weren't any at civil ceremonies, but they would make her a maid of honour, and seeing that she was the only computer literate one in the household, Donna converted her to the idea of helping her with the task of designing and printing the invitation cards for the wedding.

Barbara had already phoned up, saying she was over the moon her wayward son was about to tie the knot, adding, that even though they hadn't met Donna yet, anyone who could keep their son on the straight and narrow, deserved a Heart Of Gold medal as far as they were concerned.

Lisa heard nothing about Philip Marks, until the day she bumped into Carrol, while taking the short cut to town through the memorial park.

"He's had his comeuppance then," she said.

"Who Philip?" Lisa surmised, as talk of him was about all they had in common these days. He's in the psychiatric ward at the Penington General, had a breakdown I'm told, tried to top himself, swallowed a whole bottle of pills," she explained.

"No I didn't know, but it I think you'd agree it was always on the cards," Lisa said, trying hard to suppress her shock.

"He had it coming, the kids won't like it though, they'll miss him on the weekends, he took them out on trips regularly," Carrol said.

"Are you and Gerry still an item?" Lisa asked, trying to change the subject.

"Yes don't be surprised if you get an invite before too long, I can't wait for the big day to arrive." Carrol said, excitedly.

Lisa avoided making any further comment about Carrol's date with wedlock, instead she made excuses to be on her way, still shaken by the news.

She knew she had taught Marks a lesson but she couldn't comprehend what he had just done. It was over a week since their encounter so there was the possibility he had done it for some other reason, something entirely different, but in her heart she knew it was because she had rejected him, plus the fact his business had gone bust

She had no plans to visit him, she hadn't planned on seeing him again anyway, yet for all that she had never wanted him dead and out of the water…not that!

She resolved not to tell anyone about their decisive meeting, it was private anyway, but the peace of mind she had enjoyed the last week or so, was shattered once again.

The man was manipulating her thoughts yet again, yet she hoped he would recover, but at the same time hoping it wasn't all her down to her.

That evening Donna noticed her friend seemed to be in another world, and she asked if there was something worrying her.

Philip…Philip Marks, he's had some kind of breakdown, tried to kill himself." Lisa said.

"Good grief…never! when did this happen?" Donna asked.

"The day before yesterday, Caroll told me when I met her in town," Lisa explained.

"I knew he was strange one, but I wouldn't have thought he was up to that," her friend said.

"Do we ever know anyone, really know someone, I mean," Lisa mumbled.

"Don't you think we should give the hospital a call, after all he gave us help when we needed it," Donna suggested.

"Yes I suppose so, would you be a love and do it for me?" Lisa asked.

"No problem." Donna said, leafing through the directory.

It took a while to get through to the ward, but finally, the ward sister at the other end gave her a report.

"She said he's making progress but still sedated." Donna explained, replacing the receiver.

"Did they ask who was making the enquiry?" Lisa probed.

"No, not really I just said it was a relative, can I suggest we forget that right now

I'm getting married in two days, remember!" her friend reminded her.

"I haven't forgotten. Did Zac arrange the reception afterwards?" Lisa asked.

"I'll kill him he hasn't, he supposed to have done it on Tuesday but I found he'd been in the betting shop most of the day, I went nuclear, I don't think he'll forget so easily next time." she said.

Donna's choice of venue for the hen party, disappointed Lisa.

"Why do you want to go all the way up to the Red Lion for there's no entertainment and we'll have to get a taxi. If you're think I'm gonna drink Tonic water all night, you'd better think again," she said

"I'm doing it for my friends, Jan and Kelly, they like a touch of class," her friend said.

"Are you sure that's the real reason… you won't find someone like Steve up there now. That was a one off, it's a boring old dive nowadays days, you're not having second thoughts about tomorrow are you?"

"No of course not," she replied.

"You're getting married in the morning remember," Lisa reminded her.

"That's just sour grapes, begrudging a girl her last night of freedom." Donna chuckled.

Zac was spruced up and ready to depart for his celebration an hour before the taxi was due to arrive.

"Where you off to then?" she asked, noting how smart he looked in his Grey check sports jacket set off with his cream shirt and blood red tie.

Tapping his nose then rolling his eyes like a silent movie actor, he quipped,

"Keep your pecker out, it's my little secret, I haven't asked where you lot are going for your hen party, have I?" he quipped.

Holding the front door ajar for him she reminded him that Donna would be staying at her old address tonight, and watched him as he marched toward the bus stop at the bottom of the road, whistling something tuneless.

By the time their taxi had arrived, after collecting Jan, Kelly, Tara and Claire, four of her friends from different pick up points around town, the driver was understandably vexed.

"You said four, now suddenly it's six." he commented as Donna and her friend squashed into the front seat.

"We'll pay you double if you'll be good boy and pick us up later." she suggested, hoping he wouldn't stick to the letter of the law.

Everyone seemed visibly relieved to finally arrive at their destination.

Half way through the journey the driver had ordered the window be rolled down because Kelly had insisted she be allowed to smoke despite all the warnings to the contrary, that, along with being squashed up like tinned Mackerel, ensured that everyone had stiff necks and severely compressed joints.

Lisa paused a while outside the hotel for a moment, recalling the last time she was here, she hadn't believed those lotto officials when they spelt out how much she had won. How naïve she had been then, it felt like a lifetime ago now.

"Are you coming then or are you going to spend the rest of your evening day dreaming." Donna shouted, from the door.

She followed her friend inside, Kelly and the rest were already seated, elevated on high stools in front of the bar, as they entered.

"All the drinks are on me." Donna Marie shouted, generating a lot of interest, causing many heads to turn around. And it wasn't long before her friend had gathered an audience around herself, and the group at the bar. Giggling and laughing, reliving fun the girls had experienced working as blue coats at a popular holiday camp in the eighties.

Lisa had the distinct feeling that this party wouldn't be quite the same as some of the other hen party's she'd been invited to over the years, she was already feeling left out, so she struck up a conversation of her own with a gorgeous hunk called Jon Morrow, a young man in his late twenties, helping out behind the bar.

As the evening wore on Claire and Donna were up at the other end of the room playing pool with two young men, one of them with so many rings and pins pierced in very obvious places, that he was in danger of setting off every metal detector in the vicinity.

Tara and Kelly were arm wrestling with two middle-aged hippies in the corner, for money, judging by the pile of bank notes spread out on the table.

A half hour had passed and the scene had changed yet again, Donna was nowhere to be seen, telling Jon she wouldn't be long, she took a tour of the various rooms, looking for her.

She eventually found her friend, outside, in a clinch, with one of the pool players, nicknamed the metal man, both of them worst for drink.

He'd gone before she had time to confront him, making her wonder if he had her down as her friend's chaperone or suchlike.

"Have you forgotten what you're about to do tomorrow?" she asked her friend..

"I walked that long and winding road before... remember? I'm just making the most of my freedom while I still got some left." she slurred.

Lisa couldn't be bothered to argue any longer; instead she dragged her friend to the restaurant, and poured a litre of strong black coffee into her.

The big day had arrived.

Lisa and the kids were the first to arrive outside the registrar office, arriving twenty minutes earlier than the wedding, scheduled for eleven p.m.

There wasn't a soul to be seen anywhere, even the doors were locked.

Earlier that morning she had left Zac standing in the hall half-naked, with a towel around his midriff, cradling the phone between his jaw and shoulder, calling the florist, as he had completely forgotten to order Donna's bouquet of flowers and a half dozen button hole carnations, for the family guests that Donna had invited.

Her friend had reminded her earlier that morning from Cashmere Avenue, after insisting she'd stay there over night because, as she said 'it was bad luck to see the groom before the wedding.'

Lisa wondered if little brother would make it on time, especially since he had promised to pick up his best man outside town.

A black taxi coasted around the corner into the street and halted not far from where Lisa and the kids were standing. Before four of Donna's friends got out and approached her.

"Just saw Zac running down the high street holding a bunch of flowers with somebody chasing after him," Jan Dodd, the woman in red, reported.

"Was the one doing the chasing short bald and fat?" Lisa asked.

Heads nodded up and down in unison.

"That's his best man Norman Stanley, good old Norm! They were late I expect," she explained, not wanting to spell out his job description.

Eic, Barbara and Donna arrived next, in Eric's brand new red Fiesta; Donna looked stunning in her light blue satin suit with navy accessories.

"Where is he?" she shouted over to Lisa's direction.

"He's on his way don't worry." Kelly shouted back, with a sly wink to her friends.

Most of the people arriving, were Donna's friends from way back.

Lisa realised she didn't know many of them, taking in all the activity around her, she noticed even more cars parking up at the bottom of the road, which left her wondering why they had parked up so far away.

A group of people stormed up the road towards them and as they got closer, Lisa realised they weren't guests at all; They were obviously professional photographers, judging by the look of their expensive camera equipment.

It seemed it was her, they were after.

Donna must have sussed it out too, as she thumped and kicked the heavy oak doors of the office.

Suddenly the door creaked open a couple of inches.

A little bespectacled man peeped around at them from inside, but soon ended up straddled and jammed between the door jam and wall rebate, as the guests, spooked by all the excitement, pushed through like a herd of Wilder Beast.

"I told you this would happen, someone must have told the press I'd be here,"

Lisa said, addressing Donna as they were pushed and shoved inside the oval ceremony room lined with rows of chairs.

"Nothing's gonna happen unless that prat you call a brother turns up," her friend replied.

Zac and Norman Stanley arrived with a couple of minutes to spare, both clutching bunches of flowers, they noticed all the people with camera's too, but with the realisation that they were not all from the press, a lot of the family element in the crowd were nursing their little APSs.

Miss Rowlands the registrar, a stern looking, little woman was obviously distracted, she couldn't help turning her head towards the window every few seconds or so, wondering what all the excitement was in aid of.

"Can anyone tell me what all the fuss is about?" she quizzed, loudly.

"Well I've just been released from the big house and my best man here, who is a policeman in plain clothes, has kindly removed my handcuffs for obvious reasons." Zac joked.

Norman's head shot around like a weather vane in a storm, looking gob-smacked, Lisa tittered, and Donna was furious, her face a picture of embarrassment. Most of the twenty or so wedding guests, didn't know what to believe.

The ceremony itself was a nervous affair, the registrar, still jumpy, glancing sideways at any unusual movement outside the window, nobody thinking to tell her about the real reason the photographers were there.

Later Norman dropped the ring as he was about to hand it to Zac, and everybody in the front two rows spent a minute of so on their knees searching for it.

Kirsty found it glinting, beneath a radiator near the wall. Saving the day.

Zac had booked the reception down at Hullabaloos, a restaurant in the center of town

Lisa didn't want her presence spoiling their day any further, so she quizzed Miss Rowlands about a back entrance, if she could escape, perhaps she could get a taxi or bus and join them later she thought.

"There's a staircase which will take you down to the archives department in the basement, and the door there will lead you out to a small yard, that in turn will you exit out into Sefton Street, the street below this one." she explained.

Lisa told Donna about the escape route, and Zac offered to pick her up at the end of the road, but Lisa wouldn't have any of it.

"We'll delay the proceeding until you arrive then," her friend proposed.

"Don't you dare, this is your big day I'll get there sooner or later, don't worry,"

She waited until all the guests had arrived and followed the tiny Miss Rowlands through a dowdy green painted passageway and over to a heavy dark oak door, with ornate brass handles at the end of the corridor.

"Through here and down the stairs." she directed, holding the door open.

"Oh! by the way that man Zacarius, is he really a prisoner let out to be married?" she asked.

"No! he was just pulling your leg, it's me they are really after, the elusive lottery winner of Penington." she said, closing the door, feeling like superwoman, smiling as she descended down the dimly lit staircase.

An hour later a great cheer greeted Lisa as she entered the second floor reception room at the restaurant, she had become the center of attraction again and she didn't much like it.

They had put everything on hold until she turned up.

"What happened after you left the office?" she asked.

"Oh! Little brother here kept up the ruse of being the poor lovelorn convict, released for the day, but all they wanted to know was where you were, then when we left they followed us until Zac got the doorman here to ban them from entering, but I wouldn't mind betting there's one or two of cunning types skulking down in the bar below, waiting for the party to end." she explained.

"Well I didn't see anyone when I came in." Lisa said.

"Let's hope they've given up and gone home." Donna chortled.

"What can I say, I've spoilt your day, it would have been better if I hadn't come." Lisa said, tears clouding her eyes.

"Don't be so daft love, C'mon it's time to eat, everyone must be feel ravenous by now.

After the three course meal, Norman Stanley, who seemed to come across as the straight laced professional type, surprised everybody by turning out to be a real raconteur, rattling off anecdotes about his work, and adding the odd smutty joke here and there until, the intrusive muted trill of a mobile phone stopped him in his tracks.

Everybody in the room looked to the one sitting next to them for the source of the bell, until Zac finally fumbled inside his jacket coat and brought out his mobile.

"Hello!... Zac Tinsley here what can I do for you." he said, in a clear voice, conscious of his captive audience.

Deathly silence reigned as his one sided conversation progressed.

"I'm in the middle of my wedding." *Pause.*

"I see." *Silence.*

"Oh yes I'll tell them." *Silence.*

"Right! before I go then." P*ause.*

"Bye now."

Donna held her head in her hands, and Eric and Barbara were continuously tutting, until someone broke the mood, switching on a Karaoke machine up on the small stage, down at the front of the room.

"Why the bloody hell didn't you switch that thing off before you started, it isn't as if you're a doctor... or a plumber even," Donna shouted, cupping Zac's ear.

Lisa, curious, tried to lip-read her little brother's reply, but couldn't make any sense of it, but she heard her friend reply,

"Don't say anything now it will spoil everything."

She wondered what was so important; maybe their flight had been cancelled, or did they have trouble with the passports perhaps.

All was forgotten soon afterwards, when Zac got up on the stage and got the Karaoke started, it wasn't long before he dragged Norman up and they give a rendering of

"The Wind Beneath My Wings.'

And even Jan Dodds had a go, singing 'Climb Every Mountain.'

Pam said she was leaving and offered to take the kids, Lisa was getting worried that they were all drinking too much, she had promised to get them to Heathrow at midnight to catch the night flight to Bangkok, to start their two week long honeymoon, at the beach resort at Pattaya.

Zac was really under the weather by the time, and Norman and Lisa had dragged him off stage, Donna wasn't much better, the plan had been to go home and change before going to the airport, but now they'd only have time to pick up the suitcases.

She told Norman to look after them while she phoned for a taxi in order to get them back home to Hunters Gate to collect the Frontera.

She had only just replaced the receiver on the phone in the foyer, when there was the flash and pop of a camera.

"I've been waiting for you Mrs Whittle, tell me why are you so shy about having your picture taken, came by the ticket illegally did you?" the voice said, it's keeper slowly materializing from the shadows.

Then there was another flash, before she confronted him near the entrance doors, cracking him under the jaw with her clenched fist.

She sprinted back upstairs and met Norman and Donna coming down, having difficulty keeping her brother upright.

"The local paparazzi flashed me," Lisa said.

"Did you mange to ring for a cab?' Norman asked.

"Just about," Lisa replied.

"Show me, you just show me." Zac slurred, lifting his arm off Norman's shoulder.

"Oh! No, you don't my boy we've got a date with destiny." Donna Marie shouted, grabbing him by the collar.

Norman dashed outside, trying to catch the camera man, he must have heard or seen something, because he had bounded up the road like a greyhound chasing a rabbit.

Lisa helped her friend push Zac into the back seat and took off at speed, as Donna rolled the window down, shouting through the darkness, trying so hard to tell the elusive Norman, that they were sorry, but they'd see him when they got back.

Five minutes later they were speeding through Raydon on the outskirts of Penington when a police car came up fast behind them, lights flashing, and siren wailing. Indicating that they should pull over.

"That's done it, we'll never get to the airport on time now," Donna said peering through the rear window, watching the policeman approach.

"We must have been speeding," she added.

Suddenly Zac's eyes popped open.

"Oh! Hell, I forgot all about the old bill, I told them I'd see them before we went." he slurred, struggling to sit upright.

Lisa recognized the policeman as soon as he tapped on her window.

It was little boy blue, at least that's what Zac had called him, the same one who had asked for her autograph at the station, always perpetually grinning.

"Mrs Whittle?" he asked, as she rolled the window down. Lisa nodded impatiently.

" PC Hiscock, ma'am." he said, clocking everyone in the car

"Inspector Gutteridge sent me down to warn you about Broggi Hamilton, he didn't think Mr Tinsley had understood fully what he had said on the phone, so he sent me down to the reception at Hullabaloos, but the doorman there told me you'd gone, so I set out to follow you " the constable explained.

"Understood what?" Lisa questioned.

"Hamilton! he was apprehended late this afternoon but gave Ellen…er.. the police woman the slip, over at the new shopping precinct." he said.

"It was me… I should have told you, I forgot." Zac slurred again.

"We were too afraid to say too much really, didn't want to spoil everything, and we forgot as the evening went on," Donna chipped in.

"I'm driving my bother and his wife down to Heathrow, they only have an hour and a half before their flight leaves." Lisa explained.

"Well I'll accompany you then, but I'll have to radio in first of course, my brief is to keep an eye on you, seeing that Mr Tinsley and his wife here are off on honeymoon I'll see what the Inspector says." he said, turning about and marching back to his car.

"D'you think we should call the whole thing off, we can't leave you here on your own it wouldn't be fair," Donna suggested.

"No! I wouldn't dream of it, I'll take my chances, I don't think that idiot would be stupid enough to try anything now that the police are on to him." she said.

Hiscock must have had the green light from the inspector, Lisa thought, as his car drew alongside hers, with him waving frantically through the window, indicating that she should follow.

Heads turned abruptly at the airport as the squad car, with lights flashing and siren flashing, screamed to a screeching halt outside the front entrance of the terminal building.

PC Hiscock, complete with helmet and radio receiver blaring, helped Donna to extract the still woozy Zac from the back seat of the four track, leaving Lisa to wheel their suitcases in, on a trolley, getting soaked in a heavy down- pour.

The girl at the arrivals desk questioned if Zac was in a fit state to fly, but Hiscock's authoritative appearance seemed to help. Whether it was because they thought he was being deported or not, was debatable.

Whatever!! Both Lisa and the young constable were visibly relieved when the plane finally went on its way… disappearing through a sheet of spray from a wet runway.

CHAPTER 13

Lisa followed PC Hiscock on the relatively empty M4, all the way home, arriving there in the early hours.

The house felt even lonelier than usual as she stepped inside, wondering how the kids had fared at her Pam's next door.

She decided to bed down on the settee, but very quickly realised she couldn't sleep a wink, the slightest sound setting her mind in motion, playing tricks, conjuring up grizzly scenes from spent horror movies.

Up earlier than usual that morning, she called around next door and collected the kids, thanking her kindly neighbour once again.

As soon as she had dropped the children off at school, PC Hiscock was waiting, sitting in his squad car outside the house.

Rolling the window down, he shouted that Gutteridge would like to see her at the station.

"Do you want to go in my car or yours?" he asked.

"You go on, I'll follow, I have to do some shopping later." she replied.

The Inspector bid her good morning as soon as she entered his office, indicating she should sit opposite him the other side of the polished table.

"I've asked you 'round here to explain what's happening in regard to Hamilton…some tea?" he asked, as if suddenly becoming conscious of his initial abruptness.

"Yes please, milk but no sugar," Lisa directed.

"Ellen…er' Policewoman Arnot, recognized our Mr Hamilton at Pennies, the new shopping precinct yesterday afternoon, but he gave her the slip after agreeing to accompany her to the station." he explained.

"Yes, the constable told me about it after he stopped us last night on the way down to the airport," Lisa said.

"Well you don't need me to spell put what sort of danger you're in." he said, jumping up quickly, to answer a rap on the door.

Opening it, an attractive, dark haired young policewoman came into the room, balancing two large steaming mugs of tea on a tray.

"Thank you," he said, relieving her of one, and passing it over to Lisa.

"Actually this is the policewoman in question, PWC Arnot, she nearly convinced the tattooed man to come back to the station" he said.

Lisa nodded and smiled, as the woman turned to leave.

"Look Mrs Whittle, my advice is to keep away from the shop and your home, if it's at all possible, it seems you were right when you said you saw him before, it's worrying to think he's still down here. You can bet your bottom dollar, he's done his homework, he's bound to know where you live and work by now. Have you thought about getting away on holiday somewhere?" he quizzed.

"No not yet, but I know I'll have get my thinking cap on, I draw the line at being separated from the children though, they've experienced too much trauma as it is." she said firmly.

"I can understand that being a father myself, I'm also worried about Mr Marks, in fact I've just sent someone over to collect him, apparently he's been in hospital recently but I need to have a word with him, we haven't had chance to inform him yet.

Shortly after leaving the police station, she had only walked a short distance down the high street when she noticed PC Hiscock pull up in his car outside the building.

She couldn't help think the Inspector had got him running around like a busy district nurse.

A moment later Philip Marks got out of the car and they both walked into the building.

Instinctively she turned to meet them, then thought better of it, deciding to leave well alone, mindful of her own mounting problems.

As soon as she arrived home she checked out the answering machine, her usual feeling of trepidation intensified ten- fold, recalling the mystery calls of late, certain now, who had made them.

This time though, it was Carrol asking if she call around her place 'to hear something 'interesting' as she put it.

Curious, she decided to go over there straight away, but as she reversed the Frontera off the drive, she nearly collided with Hiscock as he pulled to a stop outside the house. It seemed the Inspector had been as good as his word sending him around two and three times a daily.

"Off out again... are you?" he called, from an open window.

"Yes! Going over to see my friend at Raydon," she replied.

"Do you mind telling me her address?" he asked.

"No of course not, it's thirty three Rossinton road, you know near St. Marks, the Catholic Church on the corner," she explained.

"I don't like asking really, but the inspector has told me to keep you in my sights at all times." he explained.

He promised to call around at least once more during the course of the day, before getting into his car and driving off down the road.

Carrol was as welcoming as ever as she opened the door, her broad cheery smile, was like a light switched on in the darkness.

"Hello darling, come on in I've got some fantastic news for you," she said turning on heel, leading the way through her long hallway.

Lisa was bursting with curiosity as she followed her into her living room.

"We've finally fixed the date for our big day, but wait for it... here's the good news, the ceremony will take place in the Seychelles five days tomorrow," she blurted out excitedly.

"That's absolutely brilliant," Lisa said, taking hold of her hand.

"If anyone deserves a fair share of happiness... you do... what made decide on the exotic?" she asked

"It was Gerry really, he's a Catholic and divorced, and when the priest found out that I was Anglican and divorced too, he told us in no uncertain terms we'd better look elsewhere, so we came up with this foreign thing, it fits the bill nicely, don't you think? The honeymoon taken care of too."

"Well I think that's a terrific idea, don't forget though, you must have a party to celebrate when you get back," Lisa suggested

Suddenly, for no particular reason, Lisa slumped down in the chair and began to cry.

"What ever is the matter?" Carrol asked, putting her arm around her shoulder.

"It's not something I've said is it? About the wedding…I mean" she quizzed.

"No nothing like that, forgive me love, I'm really happy for you, it's just that my life seems to be getting worst by the day."

She went on to explain the situation she found herself in, and her friend had difficulty believing her catalogue of sad events.

"But I thought since you had that good fortune with the lottery, everything would be plain sailing for you from then on." she said.

"It's been the opposite in fact, now I've had to move from my home, because some head case decides to get his revenge, it makes me wonder what it's all doing to the kids.

Carrol excused herself into the kitchen saying she'd make some tea, but came back in an instant, empty handed.

"The solution is staring us in the face." she said, sitting down next to her.

Lisa, still crying a little didn't say anything.

"Stay here! You can move in right away, the house is plenty big enough, when we go you could look after the place until we return," she explained.

The relief on her friend's face was obvious.

"It hadn't crossed my mind, but what about your ex?" she asked.

"I'll tell him all about it, don't worry, we planned to take the kids with us anyway, so I'll tell him there's no reason for calling around." she said.

The following days flew by. Lisa felt secure in her new safe haven, several miles from town. And at long last she finally met

Gerry Hobbs, and didn't mind admitting she felt a little envious of her friend's lucky catch, he had the looks of Robert Redford, and a personality to match.

No wonder he was a star salesman, turning on his charm, selling those tin boxes to the ladies she supposed.

PC Graham Hiscock had turned out to be real gold, after Lisa had explained her new situation, he suggested he could take the children to and fro school, and keep a beady eye on her too, 'killing two birds with one stone' as he put it.

The day finally came for Carrol and Gerry's departure, turning out to be a kind of low key affair for Lisa, she wanted to go to the airport to see them off, but they would have none of it, arguing she shouldn't take unnecessary risks, breaking her cover for the sake of a silly convention.

But after they had gone the house felt even lonelier than her own, she couldn't wait for the children to get back from school, they would miss Jack and Lowery too, she mused.

The man Broggi Hamiton was the last obstacle in her way to happiness.

She desperately wanted life to begin again, it was as if she was on the verge of being re-born. The only difference being…she had already lived a life, and knew full well what joy a happy normal life could bring

The following Friday, after his release from hospital, Philip Marks drove down into Penington to keep an appointment with Jerrold and Manning, the local estates agents in the high street.

He had brought the letter they had sent him, stating a third party had made an offer for the factory premises previously known as Marks and Whittle.

The offer price of one hundred thousand pounds was less than half than he had expected, money down the drain as far as he was concerned, he owed his creditors one and a half times that amount.

They had already confiscated his beloved BMW.

His business life was finished as far as he was concerned, and he was only too aware that his personal life was at an all time low.

Before he left he signed a form consenting to the sale, trying hard to wipe the whole bleak episode from his mind. The words of the hospital psychiatrist rang through his mind.

'Forget the hard nose business world, and find the real you. Start from there, it's the only way you are going to survive.'

The kids were the only meaningful thing left in his life, they were the only thing worth living for, so it was over to Carrol's to pick them up, then there was that trip to the park he had promised them, and a visit to the cinema afterwards so see that film they were so excited about…Harry Potter! About an adventurous boy- wizard.

The big man, his shaven head covered by a wide brimmed Panama hat, watched his quarry as he turned and left the agency office, then crossed the busy road himself, as the tall mustachioed man turned left into Needle Street to collect his car. He had bided his time spending the best part of yesterday, and a cold shivery night, hiding in the tall man's garage, adjoining his house, spending part of the time squashed up in an old steel locker. He had planned to ambush him on the first day, but that busy, young policeman had come around twice that day, checking to see if he was all right, which had solicited more and more caution on his part. He knew they were on to him, that policewoman had even called him by name, and very nearly fooled him into believing there'd been a bomb warning at the shopping at that new shopping precinct.

Pulling up the fur collar of his bomber jacket and digging his arms deeper in his pockets, he quickened his pace as he crossed over to the other side of Needle Street, managing to walk parallel with his slow walking quarry on the opposite side. Then, trusting his luck he played a game of Russian roulette with the fast moving traffic, crossing again, the same time as watching Marks get into his ancient blue Datsun. He sprinted over to the brand new Micra, a few cars behind, and followed the blue car as it took off towards the lights at the bottom of the road.

Where was he off to now? he wondered, as he closed the gap. Returning home perhaps. Whatever, he would have to make his move before long, the police were beginning to squeeze him now. He had been down south far too long anyway.

He tailed the Datsun, as it halted momentarily at the lights, before turning left into the high street, keeping up close until they had left the one way system, then he dropped back a little to allow a car come in between them, trying to disguise the obvious.

Ten minutes later the blue car indicated as it moved to the crown of the road, then turned off to the right, entering into an older district of town, a run down area of terraced houses, which reminded him of Shettleston, a similar suburban area in Glasgow. Built in the nineteenth century to house the workers, the place where he had grown up in fact.

Slowing down a little he moved further back as the Datsun turned left, entering a long street of three story bay windowed houses, up on a slight gradient. He watched as the car in front stopped, and the tall man getting out. Inching forward a little, he waited until someone had opened the door. He couldn't see who it was from where he sitting, but Marks remained there along time, perhaps he wasn't going to go inside after all, a couple of minutes later he was still there, and he wondered why. Then suddenly he was gone, now was the time to make his move, surely the police wouldn't show up this far off the beaten track, he thought.

Jumping out of the Micra he walked the ten yards or so up to the steps. Climbing them he felt inside his jacket for his switchblade, and rapped on the door. Lisa opened it, her facial expression serious after an altercation with Marks, who was adamant that Carrol hadn't told him anything about going away.

"Yes?" she asked, her eyes, immediately drawn to his unusually large Panama hat.

The big man didn't say anything, but grinned insipidly as he removed the hat slowly, at the same time as pressing the switch button on the stiletto handle.

Lisa screamed, as he gripped her shoulder and spun her around like a top, with just one movement of his huge powerful hand.

"Inside!" he shouted, cupping her mouth and pressing the blade into the small of her back.

Marks stood motionless at the end of the hallway as if caught in a time warp.

"Get in there." Broggi ordered him, prodding Lisa from behind, spinning her again, before throwing her bodily, onto the settee.

Staring straight at Marks he grinned, saying,

" I never expected this, I knew you'd lead me to her but not straight into the nest like this,"

"Now grab that curtain," he ordered.

Marks was flummoxed, not understanding what he meant.

"The curtain… the drape man… rip it down and cut it into pieces," he shouted, aggressively this time.

Lisa stabbed her finger behind Broggi's back, pointing to the sideboard drawer.

Marks slid it open and brought out a pair of scissors, then cut and ripped the materiel into four inch wide strips.

"C'mon c'mon hand them to the hen here," he barked.

"Now lucky lady tie your friend up, hands behind his back," he said, grabbing her elbow, guiding her up.

Marks turned around and crossed his wrists at the base of his back.

If Lisa had any notion about tying the bonds loosely, Broggi put paid to that, by supervising every twist and turn of the materiel.

"Sit down on the floor," he ordered, as if shouting to a dog.

The tall man literally slid down the wall and ended up lying on his side for fear of hurting his arms.

The big man forced Lisa to sit on the settee again, as he dumped himself down next to her, grabbing her wrist, and squeezing it in his vice like grip... shouting,

"Five hundred thousand! That's my price, write out a cheque, dig the money up, rob your own bank, do whatever you have to, that's my price for you and your friend's life,"

"I couldn't get my hands on that amount of money if I tried, everything is invested, all I have is three thousand in my bank-book and a couple of hundred in my current account," Lisa explained.

"Leave her alone man, can't you see she's telling you the truth," Marks shouted, from the other side of the room.

The big man jumped up and snatched up a piece of material left on the floor. Grabbing him by his hair, he slapped him on each side of his face before gagging him.

"Keep your big mouth shut, you speak when I want you to, understand!" he barked.

Lisa began to cry un-controllably.

"Crocodile tears won't work with me hen, that won't change anything…now where do you keep the hard stuff, don't you lot like the drink down here," he shouted, searching through the sideboard, before rifling a writing desk in the corner.

Lisa stood up, indicating he look in the kitchen.

"Sit down!" he growled as he walked in and brushed aside plates, pans and cutlery crashing them on to the floor, in his quest to find what he wanted.

He appeared at the door again, gulping from a large bottle of Whiskey.

Lisa prayed Hiscock would come, he usually called around once in between taking and collecting the kids from school.

The carriage clock on the mantle shelf opposite, read two twenty five, she tried to recall what time he'd come yesterday, she always gave him a wave or hand signal, but if for some reason she didn't, he'd usually knock the door for a quick chat.

Broggi slumped back down next to her on the settee again, and she wondered if the whiskey bottle had been full when he'd started, it was nearly empty now.

"Go and get me all your bank- books… everything do you understand." he ordered.

"They're upstairs in the bedroom," she explained

"Well you know where that is… don't you. Go get them, and don't be long or I'll have some fun with your friend here, shut his big mouth up forever," he growled, drawing the blade across his throat.

Lisa took a tentative step towards the door expecting him to follow, but as she climbed the stairs, he still hadn't made a move.

The temporary feeling of freedom generated a hundred escape plans in her mind's eye, but she knew any notion of escape was doomed from the start, overshadowed by what he would do to Marks.

As she grabbed her handbag off her bedside cabinet, she found herself thinking that she would willingly pay him what he asked if he would go, just disappear out of her life forever, but she had told him the truth, she was living off interest, they had advised her to invest her money that way, until she had sorted herself out, cashing anything in now, would take at least a week. And how could she explain that to someone like him? He would detain her in the house for as long as it took.

Turning to go back downstairs she caught a glimpse of something white in the street below, moving closer to the window she saw the police car, her car…it was Hiscock's car! He had stopped there, waiting for her to wave the same as yesterday, but his eyes seemed to be fixed on the bay window below her. Instinctively, she started to rap on the window, then flung her arms around like a race course bookie. The noise must have alerted Broggi, as she heard the thud of his heavy footsteps ascending the stair at speed.

"What the hell is going on up here?" he shouted, she guessed about half way up the staircase.

Lisa threw the contents of her handbag crashing to the floor, and knelt down pretending to retrieve them, as he marched in, still clutching the empty whiskey bottle.

"What's all the din about?" he asked.

" Dropped my bag that's all, I tripped," she lied, crawling around, searching underneath the dressing table.

Stepping over her he looked down to the road below, she closed her eyes in despair thinking the game was up, but he didn't say anything as he walked back to the door.

"Now move it woman before I really lose my rag," he said, clumping back downstairs again.

Lisa jumped up and looked down into the street, the car had gone, it couldn't have been there when he had looked, or there would have been hell to pay, she thought.

She wondered if Hiscock had seen her frantic movements or heard her knocking on the window- pane, as she descended the stairs

Broggi was sat at the dining table as she entered the room, he grabbed her handbag and held it up in the air, scattering the contents over it, searching for her bankbook and cards.

Glancing side eyed over to Marks still lying in a foetal position, she thought to wink, roll her eyes, screw her face up, anything! to indicate there was still hope, but she didn't dare take the chance, knowing how observant the hard man was.

The poor man had argued that Carrol hadn't told him anything about going away, but she had her doubts, it was as if he was in some kind of trance still in the throes of a nervous breakdown or something, a shadow of the man he once was.

"Three grand, three measly grand," he muttered as he scrutinized the bank- book.

"I told you that's all there is except for a couple of hundred in the current account," she said.

Suddenly, he hurled the bottle he'd been holding across the full length of the room, hitting an ornamental mirror, smashing it into myriads of pieces, some of the residue showering Marks on the floor.

"Well we're all in for a long stay then, I hope there's plenty of grub in the house 'cos I'm not leaving 'till you give me what I want," he screamed, rushing into the kitchen again, searching for the obvious.

It was the glint that caught her eye, the knife… his knife, on the table.

He was still stomping around like a wild Elephant in the kitchen, no doubt getting angrier by the second, searching for more of his elixir.

She had a split second to make up her mind, after that it would be too late.

Moving like a frightened cat she snatched it up and dived over to Marks, inserting the blade beneath the bonds, slicing through them quickly, nicking the poor man's wrist in the process, droplets of blood dripping on to the carpet below, before quickly replacing the knife back on to the table.

Seconds later Broggi appeared guzzling from a large bottle of homemade Elderberry wine he had found in the kitchen.

Lisa held her breath in case he had noticed something out of place, but he sat down at the table again sifting through more of her things.

"You and I are gonna take a wee trip to the bank for this little lot," he said, slapping her face with the bankbook.

"So I want you to be a good little girl and withdraw that cash and ask for some forms to cash in your bonds, d'you understand?"

Lisa nodded, hoping he wasn't planning to go immediately, if Hiscock had seen her there was just a chance he would bring some help before too long.

The drink was obviously have some effect on Broggi, as he stumbled and swayed over to the bay window, glancing furtively up and down the street, giving Lisa a chance to give a thumbs up sign to Marks, now facing towards her, having turned over on to his opposite side, in an attempt to hide his severed bonds

She wondered if the poor man had any inkling about PC Hiscock and the arrangement they had made.

"Is that your four-track out front?" the big man asked, looking straight ahead.

"Yes!" she replied, already chiding herself for telling him anything.

"Get your keys, we're gonna take a little trip down to the bank," he barked, turning and walking back in her direction.

Lisa didn't see the big man wobble as he tried desperately to keep his balance, coming towards her, but the firm grip of Philip's hand had already done the job it had intended, as the big man tumbled and crashed face down on the floor, directly in front of her.

She was as surprised as Broggi must have been.

Phillip Marks jumped up like a jack in the box grunting something unintelligible from beneath his gag, as he grabbed hold of a chair near the dining room table, he raised it above his head and swung it down across the middle of Broggi's back.

The shock of the impact caused the big man to arch his back, expelling air like a deflating balloon.

Lisa snatched the knife off the table again, and crouched above him as Marks wrestled to turn him over on to his back.

Suddenly, the big man's eyes opened wide, and he began to scream obscenities, flaying his legs out in every direction, he caught Marks, tripping him up and causing him to fall headlong into Lisa's arms, dropping to the floor.

Somehow, Lisa had held on to the knife, but now, Broggi and Marks were wrestling for possession of it.

The big man won, and stood up as Marks tried to repeat his stunt, grabbing his ankle to try and bring him down again, but the big man brought the blade down in an ark, and stabbed him in the chest.

Lisa struggled up on her feet, trying to stop him, but he swung his fist into her face.

And the last she remembered was spinning and falling like a stone, crashing on top of him, as he lay prostrate on his back

Everything was a mottled blue when she opened her eyelids, she soon realised her stare was fixed on the carpet three inches below her face.

She was lying horizontally across Marks who moaned continually, obviously in pain, the side of her face felt as it had, at the dentist, after an injection.

But Philip's need became her over-riding motivation now, as she thumped her elbow in to the carpet, and propelled all her weight upon it, rolling over on to her back.

She was covered in blood, its insidious crimson stain, spreading out, and down the front of her.

The full realization of what had happened came home to her.

He had stabbed Philip, and attacked her, but why hadn't the animal done something for him? there was blood everywhere.

Turning on to her stomach again she slipped her shoes off and dug her toes into the carpet, and moved up towards him, inch by painful inch, until, at last her head was facing his.

He turned his head around slowly, to face her, mumbling something inaudible.

"Don't talk now try and save your strength," she whispered, placing her hand upon his forehead.

"I love you...I've always loved you." he mumbled, his haunted eyes, expressing haste.

They were his only words before his eyes rolled back, sinking into unconsciousness.

Lisa didn't hear the crashing sound of the door being smashed in, or see the three men from the armed response team, as the enforcer used his battering ram to rush inside, after she had blacked out again.

There was no doubt, had she been conscious, she would have been surprised at how easy the big man had given up, acting like a scared child, as soon as he's been confronted by that policeman with his Heckler and Koch carbine, cowering beneath a bed.

"How long have I been here?" Lisa asked the inspector sitting next to her bed in ward nine at the Penington General Hospital.

"You were brought in late last night, but there's nothing seriously wrong, apart for a few cuts and bruises, the doctor tells me they'll be letting you go home sometime today." Gutteridge explained.

"And Philip?" she quizzed.

"Well I'm afraid there was nothing we could do for him, he didn't make it. He died shortly after we got him here," he said.

Lisa felt strangely sad, and empty hearing the news.

"Tell me how did you find out that Hamilton was in the house?" she asked.

"Graham…PC Hiscock, was the one, when he realised you hadn't responded he went up and knocked on the front door." Gutteridge explained

"Yes, I saw his car from upstairs, and tried to attract his attention, but Broggi threatened us with the knife and told us to keep quiet," Lisa interrupted

"The constable realised something was wrong, as your car was still outside, so he moved down the street a little, to keep an eye on the house, then he saw the blue Micra, that hired car, parked a couple of doors away. The same one he'd seen parked up outside Mr. Mark's house, earlier on in the week, he'd made a note of the number then. Thinking it was too much of a coincidence; he hi-tailed it back to the station.

That boy will be in line for promotion after this." he elaborated.

"He didn't see me at the bedroom window then?" Lisa asked.

"No I don't believe so," the Inspector said.

Just as he finished speaking, a female doctor appeared as if from nowhere, and asked her how she felt.

"There's nothing broken, so if you feel up to it you can go home this morning, if you want." she added.

"Just give me the chance, and I'll be off," Lisa said.

Gutteridge stood up buttoning up his stiff, navy Mackintosh.

"Call me when you feel up to it, there's no hurry." he said, before bidding her farewell, turning, then disappearing through the double doors.

The doors hadn't swung back into place before Pam appeared, carrying Ben, with Kirsty in tow, tugging at her hand.

Lisa didn't wait for them to approach as she jumped out of bed to meet them, hugging and kissing them both in turn, much to the young doctor's disapproval.

For the first time in a long- long time Lisa felt happy and secure, even though she was aware she had an inquisitive audience witnessing all the drama, from both sides of the ward

Less than an hour later, they were on the way home in Pam's car.

Lisa asked her if she could make a detour to the cemetery, she wanted to see Martyn's new head stone. She hadn't had a chance to see it

Pam and the children remained in the car, while she walked through the drizzle to his grave.

Kneeling down at the marble headstone, she sobbed and whispered,

"I'm back my darling, I'm back, I've got so much to tell you, you won't believe it!…"

EPILOGUE

A year later, almost to the day, life had changed for everyone. Zac running the shop single-handed these days, as Donna has her hands full, Literally that is! Busy tendering to their eight-month-old baby. A beautiful brown-eyed boy, named Ben.

Over on the other side of town, Carrol is expecting too! Their new addition to the family should be due sometime in the middle of April next year.

Gerry and the children are over the moon, already playing guessing games as to what gender it will be.

Lisa? Well she's moved on, just like she said she would, but not too far away.

Only four miles outside town in fact, to a tastefully converted, nineteenth century Victorian vicarage, with eight bedrooms, four bathrooms, and a very special room. Already decorated, and set aside for a nursery, just in case.

And these days, she's not alone. Moved in with Jon!... do you remember him?

The good- looking, young barman, who gave her safe refuge at Donna's awful hen party at the Red Lion, the country pub that figured so much in her life

Kirsty is attending Berringham boarding school, two dozen miles away, so she manages to come home every weekend, and little Ben has made a lot of new friends at his new village primary school.

Lisa still makes her weekly pilgrimage to the cemetery to talk to her beloved Martyn, Telling him about everything that has happened in her life, and recently, for the first time, she made her way over to the garden of remembrance, to place a single red rose on Philip Mark's plot.

Incidentally, the villain big Broggi Hamilton, has joined his old friends in the big house at Berlinne... this time though, he will be a guest of her majesty for life.

Some would say, all's well that ends well, and I'm sure Lisa would be the first to agree. But there are times, especially when she is alone in her room, when she would willingly give up her pot of gold, for those innocent days… days of glory, when she and Martyn had fallen headlong into a special place called love.

But that was in a different time in another world.

Shield  Crest

www.ingramcontent.com/pod-product-compliance
Ingram Content Group UK Ltd.
Pitfield, Milton Keynes, MK11 3LW, UK
UKHW041437180426
11947UKWH00007B/494